Also by John Fraser

and published by AESOP Modern:

Animal Tales

Black Masks

Blue Light / Starting Over

The Case

Down from the Stars

Enterprising Women

Hard Places

An Illusion of Sun

The Magnificent Wurlitzer

Medusa

Military Roads

The Observatory

The Other Shore

The Red Tank

Soft Landing

The Storm

Three Beauties

Wayfaring

RUNNI

RUNNERS

John Fraser

'…. we run because we like it
Through the broad bright land.'

Charles Hamilton Sorley (1895–1915)
The Song of the Ungirt Runners

AESOP Modern Fiction
Oxford

AESOP Modern Fiction
An imprint of AESOP Publications
Martin Noble Editorial / AESOP
28 Abberbury Road, Oxford OX4 4ES, UK
www.mne-aesop.com

First edition published by AESOP Publications

A catalogue record of this book is available from the British Library.

First edition 2010, revised 2014

ISBN: 978-0-9561409-6-8

Printed and bound in Great Britain by
Lightning Source UK Ltd,
Chapter House, Pitfield, Kiln Farm,
Milton Keynes MK11 3LW

Contents

1 Runners in Training

LOOKING AT pictures (escorted by armed men).

The wise athletic fish leaps, and topples down the fisherman. We move along. From the millstones, tiny warriors in blue armour spill out.

Someone nearby is playing ping-pong. There is perfect peace. I can see the plantations through the plate glass, too stuffed with sun they seem, the plants can't nod with no wind – but the filtered scent is lulling. Midsummer. Satyrs, druggy decadence, and peace – for this slice of time – is perfect.

The ping-pong's more insistent, and my counsellor, Shapur, says, 'Get the fuck down!' – we're all asprawl each other, a kind of terrified orgy – me and Shapur, the lady spy, Lili, and

Rick who will succeed me. A fine quintet, end of act one, all horizontal.

'Some guy is popping at us' – maybe the guy that's grown those too green plants, the flowers already on the edge of rot. It's someone else's territory, or even faith, a state in travail. We're pinned down, and then we hear the helicopter, and we think 'we're saved', but no, it's rattled off. It's like those solitary wasplike things, so finicky about their nesting, just buzz around, out on house hunts.

When we've all settled down again, our situation's bad. Wrong orders given, guys get killed – I only bought this job, I'm not elected, just got lucky with the cards. I'm the one responsible for all the guys that's killed, but not responsible for being killed.

We scuttle out. Sara, the lady spy, has brought her hammered car, her Hummer, a military look, no windows and no armour. We all jump in, the pictures in the show have left us with their violence, not tranquillity – the fish, the mill.

We're all scared stupid. Our paid friends, with guns, have left.

*

I hear, 'The dead ones climbed up to help the strangled ones.'

We're huddled here, but I stand up. I'm the politician, after all, although I'm not elected, not responsible. I wave my arms. There's a militiaman, aims high, down come some leaves, a fruit, a body arches up, and Shapur says, 'No one's gonna vote for you now', and in the trees we see them, dangling or supine, lying along the branches, like apples on a paradise tree or sleeping jaguars. The hanged ones dance the *pizzica*, a courtly dance, a-circling back to back in couples, each Jack with a Jill, resolute, and concentrating.

A big guy, fireman maybe, says 'Outathere', and now they pull me out, I'm being hawsered, face down and screaming, along the ground, my pants is halfway off, more worrying than all the oil and roots and such – that head gouge feels quite deep – my friends are shouting 'stop', but everything is speeding up, we've lost slow-time, when life is fitted up in beige, no more cascades of blood and prick of cordite.

'Why'd you winch him away?' screams Lili. 'He's our big coin, gets us away from all these fucking indigenes,' and I know she means the Indians, our Mayans. Or suchlike. She is our athlete, long white legs that scissor past her rivals, will go far and fast, though not as fast as me – I'm planing over rocks and half my face is gone. I hope it was the ugly half, and laugh.

*

Later, I say, 'The massacre I stumbled on, indigenous guys?'

'So-called,' Shapur explains. 'They've been shovelled over the border. . .

'Well,' I say, wisely, 'we must all be

indigenous somewhere.'

'And they got cash, for being killed, and not ungrateful either.'

'Got those little telephones that everybody uses?'

'As usual, responsibilities elude us,' Shapur concludes, 'though yours seemed plain enough. We'll have you take a holiday, then maybe have you win election, clear the slate. When there's a plot, and tit for tat, the most important thing is that your tit should televise as tat.'

I'm innocent, though innocence in adults makes you look a fool.

*

'Meanwhile,' Shapur says, 'we'll think of your successors—'

'I've only just arrived.'

'Already there's been a massacre, then they shoot at you. And Sara's there on hand with transport. You are perishable goods, my friend.'

'Who's in the frame?' I say grumpily.

He shows a photo. Lili. Long legs. 'Ran in the Olympics. Makes them very popular.'

'That's all she can do, just run? Some hunting, maybe, even gathering? And did she win?'

'No, maybe some other time. An also ran. And, speaking quite humanistically, she's unspent coin.' He looks me up and down. 'Running's important in this job.'

'We take on Lili, then,' I say, 'like that Greek girl that dropped her apple. And after? Her being the dessert?'

'I think some muscle. A beautiful boy, he's done TV, told all he thought to millions, and it wasn't much, but here he is.'

Rick. One of those limping heroes of the Greeks, somewhat a bully boy.

'Security is what they want,' Shapur says. 'People. Sit safely in the evenings.'

'Watching us,' I say. 'But how's their security assured, assuming they've a place to sit?'

'Security means breaking heads. And legs too, if you must. Even give brains a little tweak – channel dire thoughts away, access to information, that's the thing.'

'So, he's the thug that specialises in chop and change?' I say.

'That is what security is all about, roughing people up, and he's the man. You can't rely on lady spies with little trucks to get you out of messes. Eternal peace, yes, that's the goal.'

'It's perfect peace. That is the phrase, remember it.'

So, there's the crown prince and the princess. Both beautiful, and satisfied, one with the other.

*

Escape, and cure. Then, I have this letter from my poor friend. Things got better, for he died, or should have.

He writes, 'Poverty is one thing. I'm destitute, which is another. Don't send me cash – I've no address, no document to claim it with. Poverty is walking uphill, with bricks balanced on your head. Destitution – the bricks have fallen, you can't sell the pieces, you sit surrounded by their crumbs.

'Worst of all is being without summer clothes, you have to wear your winter wardrobe all the year. Cell for a night – is something, but you want permanence: permanence is paradise or hell, but better than this earthly life, so small – and yet you don't feel ascetic, spiritual. A begging bowl would be a luxury, you use a plastic cup that's dirty with some curds of sour . . .'

And he goes on, it's rather sad, but he had the time, the paper too – a find one day! The stamp! I'm glad for him.

‘Even in extremes there’s hope’, Shapur says, and I think ‘hohum’ but don’t say.

‘. . . The bank was not my problem. The heat, my sweat, filled my thick trousers with what clung like treacle. Some brandy clogged my tongue and sent my brain on helter-skelter.

‘The bank guy said, “Nah, moussyurrr, you ain’t got naw bucks.”

‘My Spanish and my Portuguese twirled out, like two ingredients of a sauce. “Naw. Naw bucks.”

‘Someone impatient in the line behind said, “You must ask your country for some money,” and I almost shout, “The buggers expelled me,” but the bank guy said, “extradition”. From the rear comes “terrorist”, but I hear “heist”.

‘Poverty is dull. Eyes down for a chance find, some coin, ice cream not melted out, eyes down so’s not to meet the others’ eyes especially cops’ eyes – so quick to take offence. To sleep, to dream in someone’s car, you can’t stretch out, this goddam clean green obsession – oh where are those old Strato Chiefs . . . These pants, no cash to lose through holes, but never taken off, you smell so fruity, like beef stew, the nearest that you get.

'But this won't last. The priests, even the Sufis, tell you that. For you get ill, or find a scam. Or even rob a guy, and if he doesn't shoot, you pay off your debts and make some more. Find some sect, militia, or a gang, that lets you live.

'I saw an Ecuadorian passport. In a pile of leavings, most of the middle was ripped out. The holder looks wolflike, red gums, red eyeholes, and dark lips. I picked it up and had it hidden. You never know. Fortune favours a mathematician, so they say.

'This isn't where the story starts.

'It started when I wrote, "finding various selves. In greenhouse, forest, zoo, aquarium. Broken clay sickles in the sand, the palaces blown off, away – only the winged animals endure, in sandstone. Burial scenes.

'"I choose my drugs quite carefully. Effects unknown, but mixed with care. Fifteen seconds in the bar, and swig it down. It's always revolution, burning ramparts in the streets, the traffic is De Sotos, Packards, where the hell we find ourselves? – and what's to come, thoughts luminescent, angry, desperate. Tripping up and down, motions of dervishes, everything is twirling and will bring forth – something. Shooting them down, dismembering and hanging, then the pauses, years stretched out in antechambers, waiting for nameless empires to collapse, emit a sentence, give their resignations. All into skulls."

'When my wife finds this I say, "It's just writing, doesn't change a thing. And I'm so careful with the substances."

'She says, "That's why you're such a freak in bed," and I say, "Yes, it's true, sex is impossible and laughable, all those half-cooked people on the sheets."'

*

'It was Sonya, my wife's friend. Called the cops. There, I'm in court. The judge says, "I've got the punishment all prepared – finding the crime I'm having difficulty..." and I'm quite fascinated and I say, "Depends what you want the punishment to do. Night sweats, protect me, change me – protect you? Or is just being bad enough to deserve a punishment? But being bad's a punishment, we're told. Or maybe being weak, concealing blackmailers – how the hell you'd know? Or transpose me to another level of reality, less visible, not Thing in itself, but just The Thing."

'I giggled, thinking of a prisoners' jail, a board outside that says The Thing. The judge is thoughtful, thinking of his lunch, and I of mine, but no, it seems I'm being put away, the question is, how long? An hour? It seems interminable. A month? – you'd never notice. A year? – begins to grind, but you've forgotten everything, and there's company, prisoners, warders, just like school . . . Well, what a fate, what tasks, unless you are an angel or a devil, shapeshifting and moral glue required to see you through, I start to talk about morality, but then the Judge says – "Take him off – until the jasmine loses scent," I must have heard him wrong, the cop beside me says, "That's huge," and to his mate says, "Well, that's goodbye to this one!" and they take me off.

'The door has been left open, they don't think condemned men just walk out. That's what I do, I have a beer or two, and no one comes to hook me out, they've got enough in every cell, another one would be a growth, a cancer messing it all up. I leave the pub, I walk, I run away.

'I get to this strange country here. Everything is easy, all that lacks is cash. It's very difficult. All that lacks is cash.'

*

My poor deluded innocent friend. I wave the letter at Sara. And her short, sharp cheroots. Smoking them's like driving nails right through your tongue.

'I like a hot smoke,' she says. Unkissable.

'The moral is,' she says, 'don't escape unless you've money. Moralists don't look forward to the last chapter, yet they should. Dying, though, it solves the "how long" problem, and the "what for". All that.'

'No one gets jailed for using drugs,' I say, 'going primeval, to find a personality by multiplication – locking him up, it makes no sense.'

'Well,' she says, with authority, 'justice is one size fits all, or else it wouldn't be justice. It would be narrative, just literature. One thing before another, and anyway, the guy is dead, and probably beyond our aid.'

So, Sonya gave him to the law, redressing the misery he'd maybe caused his wife. Notion from Greek theatre – except the law had no use for him and spat him out. The rest was fortune. Useful thing to have, fortune: fatal without. Without, means choice of wrong fire exit, all excavated characters junked into one, and under necessity like a vice. Fantasy into owl's pellet. Worthless.

But his is not my story. Sara says, 'Your mistake – those people swinging from the trees, or lying supine, as you say, like sleeping jaguars – it's not displeased us. You can still go far. And soon you will. We'll find a way to send you off, the slate will fade and clean, you get experience of this and that, mostly abroad. Then you come back. As candidate.'

'Sounds good,' I say.

*

'If they, if we, decide to run you,' Shapur says, 'you must promise liberalism, take what money is offered, and off you ride – ride with the waves.'

'So far so good,' I say, 'it's free for all, but

what about these successors, Lili and Rick, the doll, the macho cop? And that little wizened, fumicated harpie, Sara, on hand in the countryside when things turn out difficult, as they always do?'

'Cast a cold eye,' he says. 'In general, do what you can and don't feel guilty.'

'All these other guys, want to make their history on us.'

'Can't stop them carrying bags of ideals collected in their past,' he says.

'Ideals is one thing, armies is another. Shooting should be occasional. After my mistake, I keep my thumb out of people's eyes.'

He pushes on. 'Brush up your rhetoric. Quips that adhere and last.'

I stare. I try to weigh his words. Really, I want atonement, mercy – not forgiveness, not election.

'The world is round again,' he says, 'a fine discovery. Democracy is something understood the most where they don't have it.'

*

I try out my speech. 'I rule, quite benevolently, over a newly ordered, chivalrous country.' No!

'I rule, quite bloodily, over a country besieged, implacably divided. Enemy languages I can't speak.' No!

'I govern, by accommodation, a small country, really a city with its periphery. Really, a large village, pigs in the streets, one house only with a garden, and a lawnmower.'

Should never have signed those dodgy papers, made that call. Wouldn't want militiamen in my stables. No, of course I don't have stables.

Chivalry. Becoming elected mayor, committees of wise guys, know how it all works, blood into manhattans, flypast of old planes, poets honoured, new little battleship on the lake, fucking waste of money, that. Who's for dinner? mad monks and horseless generals – the bottom table. Need a taster, spit it out into your lap, give prizes for some artwork, copied from somewhere, ancestors' folios raided, Mayans did or do it better – those sacred caves, full of bones and on the walls incised the little dancing men, skewering the beasts.

*

In fact, I'm not elected, I bought the deputy mayorship while the top guy was on holiday. My big mistake, those paramilitaries.

*

'Repentance,' says Shapur, is too strong. 'Your public wants you to reflect, no more. And have a private income.'

'I don't have a public.'

'That's why we'll run you, to find you

one.'

'I represent nothing.'

'Then you'll do fine for minorities, besides, you won't have to deal in votes – you'll just make decisions, quite another thing.'

And so, and so, and on and on.

*

My little guilty party leaves, we're into our first run!

Countries are a wonderful discovery. You take the plane, countries transform you from a pariah to a refugee, and then to saviour. Here, they're all old: there, all young. Here smog: there desert. Wonderful.

I go to the tobacconist's kiosk, musing on chance and destiny.

The guy in the kiosk seems a dwarf, but I've seen him, stretched, outside. He's tall, a beanstalk. He indicates the sign, 'ciggies while u can'.

'To pass the time,' he laughs.

I've no money. I'm waiting for a win.

He presses on, 'You want Gold Tips? Some Cravens? Geetarnz? Pappyrosy?'

(Sara is here, oh no, I think, when I find out. Maybe a gift?) – I say, 'Maybe cheroots.'

'Luckies? Want Luckies? Better chance with them.'

'Cheroots.'

He digs them out, they're flaking, like cocoons long dried, dead fingers that will never talk. He crumbles one.

'Seen better times,' he says. 'The lady too.'

I wonder if he's sure that, yes, her times were better. Earlier at least. I turn away, I think I hear a cackle – rare sound these days. When I am out of sight, I bin the smokes – I haven't paid, he hasn't asked.

Of course! He's in a lookout post, they put him there, then move him on, that kiosk full of wasted warehouse stuff. Contraband? Mafia?

Spy? The kiosk portable, him doubled up all day, waiting for promotion.

More ads. 'People wanted, strong but shallow.'

'Surely you knew,' Sara says, 'you called the cops to move the nomads on, the cops just call the army, for the soldiers this is quite beneath them – Mayans! – so the paramilitaries come, and there'd be deaths, a kid will tell you that. You didn't know? What are you, some upcountry mayor?'

Well, deputy. Not elected. Yes, I guess I knew, I know. A sin against my intelligence.

In the line, there are two Polish soldiers, ahead of me, and hand in hand. Playing the horses in Poland. They wear tall conical hats – material that looks like carpeting. There is a sign – 'This week, two hundred million', and I think, Back home it takes you months, embezzling a sum like that, and I am in my mind again, back with the tribes, aggression, the sacred rites that seem to mean so much, those lovely animals too, all sacrificed. The priests so kindly, catching blood. Indigenous with their little telephones, they talk all day on them. They think that then – they were all free. And now – free too. Absurd that I should take it personally.

It is my turn, I play accumulators on the Krakow hippodrome.

'Come along,' the guy behind the glass says, 'it's only virtual, no racing there for years.'

The Polish boys are giggling, they're both around fourteen. 'Best job ever, this soldiering,' they say, and I think, not if your number's up.

'Hope your number's up,' they say, and I reply, 'You're off to fight, then' – pleasantly, though that is not my character.

'We're proud to have the call,' they say, and armies are the place to take your lover, like the monasteries until the locals burnt them down ('those homos living high'), and looted. So, once we had the wandering monks, and now disbanded soldiery, and musing so and so, in a few days, I visit my tobacconist.

'Hey – you got lucky numbers!' he says.

'Millions?' and I laugh.

'Lots.'

'I'll take them in this bin bag.'

'Not from me, you won't.'

'What must I do?'

'Go to the source.'

'Poland? Krakow?'

'I told you. No horses. Numbers.'

It's a puzzle. Not yet a mystery.

'Well, it's reward for the horses,' he says.

'Well, really it's an insult.'

Better, though, to be a winner than to have done the unmentionable. The unforgivable.

*

I use a credit card to buy me – the course in Enlightenment. They give you food as well.

I use it too to buy a guy a ticket for the bus to

Krakow, to pick up all I've won. I promise him an embassy when he gets back.

*

Well,' the Leader says, 'You all got some meaning out of that?' and we all nod or sniff.

'You see the link,' he goes on, 'via Alexander, who didn't make it – quite – into the Punjab, now his Macedonians dig away beside Punjabis. Creative endeavours flourish,' and he beams. 'Though to destroy that mediocre landscape's a disgrace – for we all know that to destroy a thing of beauty is quite reprehensible. A thing that's mediocre – that's much much worse.'

A guy that we call Pliny says, 'Those diggers – presence is quite gratuitous, their origins submerged by need to skeeter though the world to send home cash . . .'

The Leader interrupts. 'Gratuitous gratuities. The waiter says – "Without my gratuities, I'd be on basic wage." The "meaning", friend? To some, a lemma's much the same as lemurs. Are you sure you drain the whole, thick meaning from . . .?'

2 The Course

IT'S SUGARY stuff, all spirit and longing. I doodle the Leader as various birds, but he's a short-arsed type, I don't see him as a chaffinch. I draw him female, but this makes him a shapeshifter, I don't think he has it in him.

Then, his tone changes. His face which just seems dirty, now turns darker.

'Now we can start again,' he says.

He mentions a couple of the Etruscan gods, their names and attributes vague, but I think they were just so, just like that. Undetermined Then, we tumble into full *candomblé* – I remember those Brazilian, those African deities. I have the song, the Seventies it was, an old vinyl. And on and on, and maybe something's taking shape, a rustle of old vines, maybe a snake, a little purple dust. The group is one, he says.

'Here we are – there's something you have lost, and search for intermittently. It's here, returned! It welcomes, it's the end of the world, justice and punishment, extinction and ecstasy. Not reason, that's inside us all, but a thing to apprehend, to use. It's the end and beginning,' and I think, but there's nothing there, nothing has occurred, just more dust, more air.

The final scene, the curtain will come down, we'll all go home, and Sara – yes, she's come along – gives a little jog like when she needs a smoke and all that power. . . Can make them have a revolution, go on pilgrimage, 'lock up our wives or have them all in common'.

Now – all that power is over, finished. Here we are, unmoved. Locked in our brains we are, perhaps we curse intelligence, our knowledge – but still we are immune. We are not moved, we are immobilised. Maybe we make a little shrine at home, but that is it. The power has gone, postponing the end, that's what the big cheeses say.

'You've made it all up,' says Sara, quite amused.

*

You seek – truth, enlightenment. But what if you couldn't tell the truth if it . . . Enlightenment! Do you know what it is, if you've got it? Maybe it fades, or runs away.

'That's a plummy guy, the Leader,' says Sara.

Spirituality. No, Enlightenment. Another word for true, then. The universe, disorderly. Swarming with bumps and explosions – disappearances by night, the storms of little buzzy things. Maybe another creator picks it up – a mathematician. Order. Nothing. Strikes totality like a match, needs us to worship Him. Match flares, we're off again. When you're a corpse, though, even two and two don't make much sense.

Before us there were titans – built walls and

pyramids. Obsessed and stupid – not like us weedy little brainsticks, inventing gods who need six arms to do the work of one. The friendly giants, with no machines – where'd they end up, carrying off their nymphs from canebreaks?

*

I see a heron in the pond. Battleship grey. And there's a lone flamingo – makes me think 'flamenco dancers', under those skirts perhaps pink scaly legs. The Leader sees me.

'Fine thinking going there,' he laughs, smarming with the group.

'Thank you,' I say. They laugh at me.

Then Sara, face and body fully used, smoking a sharp cheroot – 'Why can't I give them up,' she says. Like driving nails through your tongue.

The Course. Six of us, seeking some spiritual thrust. All expelled from other places, breakdowns indulged or fought, all disciples commonplace.

The poet, Marco, twists about, sliding some locution, some big fish, onto his hook: ‘After this epiphany, we should make a pilgrimage, get out of this loop.’

But there’s no epiphany, just the road, gas stations, fried-egg sandwiches, moots of flies in motels. Only when the money’s gone, the real adventures start.

My friend Sam says, ‘You think I’m superficial?’ and at once goes on, ‘Morals are the scaffolding we sometimes hang ourselves from. We think they’re for holding up the structure, really it’s for repairs, for maintenance.’

‘When Napoleon standardised the metre,’ I say, ‘he didn’t build with metre sticks. Buildings fall down, whether built in metres or in cubits.’

‘Rights are your metre sticks,’ Sam says.

*

We amble, amble, wander, trot, as it comes to each, across the plain, crisscrossed with scars of peat and black-brown water looking oily, here and there a bubble – some process unrevealed. Preservation of bodies, knitwear, cairngorms.

'We're looking for artworks,' the Leader shouts.

'That's a Toyota rad,' puffs Sam. 'Surely that's not . . .'

Then we see it – the activity. Nice yellow diggers and a crane that's finding rocks. A crew of – are they Macedonians? and there's Punjabis, you find them everywhere there's culture being made. There's the artist, looking smaller than the rest. Sits on a purplish rise, there's dead gorse, I see toadstools, looks like a dumped forest scene, Hansel and Gretel maybe, operatic waste.

It's immense, the tamga, tribal sign, Tibetan letter – cut in dark trenches in the dark. Must be a kilometre long and just as wide. And lined with cans. Could it be food? – that gesture! Or empties? – that rhetoric!

'It's orange paint,' the artist says. 'We shan't open it. Some I left here years ago, now I've the cash to finish everything.'

Sam shakes a can – inside, a solid lump sounds sullen as he rattles it.

'There's no tribe here. And no Tibet,' says Sara angrily, and will not be appeased.

The artist says, the Leader nods, 'Fullness and industry in the void. The tribes have gone – we cut out just their signs, not language.'

'A false archaeology?' I ask. 'But that's been done before, and documented . . .'

'No, no,' the artist shouts. The diggers make a noise like baboons – fighting or discussing, 'Not minimalism, that crap. The life, the vital element, is here. It's me. Or you! It's real because it's looked at. When we're not here, there's still Punjabis. One world, you see. It happens that – here, is Tibet – but all, every thing, is co-present. And when the Punjabis go on leave, the Macedonians stand on guard.'

We mill about, drop comments here and there.

‘It’s a mystery,’ Sam says, ‘not what he does, but what it’s doing here when we are here. At rest. Dead paint.’

‘It isn’t doing much,’ I say, ‘and nor are we. Together, we’re just expended labour power.’

‘And underpaid at that,’ adds a Punjabi, but he doesn’t seem to mind, for after all, it’s culture.

‘Those cans,’ I say, ‘as they rust, will disappear into the colour of the peat.’

*

They’re after Sam – he’s running. Faster than the rest of us,

‘I really need Enlightenment,’ he says.

‘Will they really kill you?’

‘That’s something they’ll enjoy.

Pliny pulls his jacket tighter round him and sniffs louder. A while ago he said, 'My young self's old, but it's not wise, my old self feels quite young, but is it wise?'

The Leader scoffs. 'No dream of action there! He seeks the fool's moon, bottom of the well. A scribbler! Orator! We look beneath the real . . .' and so and so. And now we call him Pliny, the younger and the elder, two persons in one flesh, unwholesome.

In the next room we hear the singing course swell to a roar, 'Slava, Slava Bogu.'

'Bloody people,' says the Leader. 'That crass racket, when we're nearly there.'

I think: the course is over, and we see the next batch hovering outside. They're wearing shrouds, it could be plastic macs. Waiting for their begging bowl of truth, could be Enlightenment, one size fits all, or could be custom built.

'A farewell kiss,' the Leader says, 'if not of peace, then comprehension. Remember, hatred's toxic, but remember too – don't let the buggers do you down,' and we are on our feet, avoiding Pliny, who is tough to have to kiss, and I seize Sara, who is not so keen, and kissing her's like going down to medieval hell, the smoke is black, there's stuff that's very dead.

'I hadn't thought we'd finish up so soon,' Sam says, 'now it's back to hiding from those guys,' and we all have lost some safety, refuge, which I guess is what the Leader meant – take your minds off horrors that await outside. Mine off in the past, Sam's knife or bullet yet to come.

Sara makes the horrors and then hides from them, the goddam happenstance that takes up time and gives no solace. Shards of time, the dragging hours, and then martinis or it may be yoga, visiting the sick – fuck, I don't care.

I have my fear, terrible things now done and still to come, ambition pushing and Shapur is pulling on, and Rick and Lili too, my heart is drums and pistons, black wings over eyes and ears.

We pass the new bunch, like when the movie ends, you hustle out, don't crack expression, or give a sign – though easy it would be to whisper 'crap', or 'flying high tonight'.

But no, deny them, start all over.

The Leader takes a drink, his cloak flaps round him like a pair of wings, and we go back, back to the outside, back where the gods' wrath, or indifference, makes us grin like angry monkeys.

*

A date with Maya – as we call her – from the course! At last! I feel the energy. 'Let's clean our mouths out, with some bottles of Nebbiolo,' I say, and think of dusty farmers gratefully.

'Too much?' and when we've done that, 'Drink bores are such bores,' I say.

'No, absolutely,' she says and she's crunching down some scrappy things that look like burnt monkey paws.

'"I drink down in long draughts, the wine of remembrance"' I say, 'no offence, of course,' and we drink, down the alphabet, at G, bottles of Gamza, then to Krk.

'The owner brought the Krk back personally,' I say, and Maya says how foreign literature and foreign wine to her appear the real, exotic stuff, though mixing red and white is out. I make a joke – I think, political.

She doesn't grasp it, and she tells the waiter, 'Nothing we have to do ourselves,' no cooking at the table.

'No animals,' I say.

They wheel the little carcasses off, and as they go I take a scrape of sauce, it isn't bad, but orange, yellow, sticky like it's made with blood. Raki is called for – so I call, and she calls too, we're like two swans, a swan duet. It doesn't last, the song is done – the swans fly off.

She's quite presentable, but I explain, the

sex stuff's past, and she explains how some old guys write operas when they're ancient. We think of those great raggy mops of hair, rising above the orchestra when it's over, of painters with their pants all blobbed with paint and gaping too, forgetfulness or just worn out. We giggle, life goes rattling on, the waiter's shift is nearly done and so are we. We must have eaten too, the bill is quite impressive, maybe some English marrows, so bland they might not even be – flown to the kitchen as we entered.

'You sure fucked up with those deaths,' Maya says.

'Sooner or later,' I say, 'it would have happened anyway,' and she says that's awful but quite funny too, and I see she doesn't care a fuck.

Anyway, we can't leave without tequila, grappa with rue, maybe, and I think 'rueful', but don't say. In general, the evening's giving me a boost, and then there's after, and after that as well, and I am like a tiger, or at least a cat, and curl up, lovely, quite domestic too.

*

We're all here, piled up.

I hear Rick ask, 'Where'd he get our card? D'you hide it in the sugar?' – with contempt.

'That big can of orange paint,' Lili replies. 'No one would look in there. It was on special.'

They've found my dinner bill. They talk about me.

'What's with him – he's got borderline personality?'

'You mean he's sick, with living in this room? He can't flash our cash around, best keep him short. Besides, he almost isn't here.'

'He thinks that getting votes,' Rick says, 'being a candidate – is all a kind of chrism. Doesn't see the machinery, and how it grinds.'

Lili pauses, then, 'He wants to get a Hummer.'

Rick says, 'That lump that Sara had? I thought it was all hammered out, but they was boiler plates, tacked on. Coming at you, it looked a hostile kind of ant. Used to draw machines like that when I was six – I should've made a fortune.'

'So, he wants a Hummer now,' says Shapur grimly. 'Sometimes – he's a beardless warrior, sometimes a guy too venerable for sex. It's pitiful. And where have our friends gone? We're threshing here like – like squids in a barrel! It's not easy. Firing him up, stopping him stealing. Nothing's easy – being Popeye, or a mercenary in Babylon – you've to expect some blows. Unless you want to work the fields and die at thirty. Better to take the risk, of burning at the stake, stuck like a pig, hunted and strangled like a badger. Better committed than conscripted. Instead – he wants Illumination.'

*

Sam is sweaty, blobby, you can't blame him. I want to talk about his assassins, but impatiently he says, 'The artist, performance artist, what you call him – he knows the Mongols took lots from the Tibetans, even, especially, the horrid things. Magnificent empire, the Tibetan. The scenery alone. Boring places too, of course.' He disappears behind his eyes, thinking the past.

'So,' he goes on, 'the gentle Tibetans, haha, passed their symbols to the Mongols, also their cavalry. It's all symbols, though the cavalry is real. If you've got a sharp weapon, you'll end up using it. No big idea.'

He is potting centuries. I try to join him, 'The weapon? You mean, the thing that you'll be remembered by?'

'Well, naturally, you can fight your day, and then retire – but everyone will bully you.' He seems sad. 'Scarring the hillside, that's quite a decisive thing,' and he's back among the paint cans. 'If you fill the whole lot in, you'll make a bigger mark than him. Emphasise the scar still more.'

'And your death?' I ask.

'I have to see how that fits in. It will, I'm sure, it being co-present with the larger purposes around.' I question with my face, but he stares back, and neither of us shows what purposes these are. He got in between Israel and Palestine, I think, maybe with some back-family Jewish, I don't know.

'I'm not a poor innocent, you know,' he says, and that's his luck.

'I'll see you when I've jumped a few more ships of fools,' he says, pushing on and away. He too is limping, and he says, 'Bus in Damascus. Hurt my back. Epiphany.'

Sam has now gone, but Pliny hangs around. He wears suit coats, with jeans.

'Did you wear out all the trousers, sitting with heavy brainwork?' I ask him, but he says, 'My tailor. When his clients fatten up, he widens their pants but not the jackets, so these pass to me.' Forever thin, forever solipsistic. But there's style with him.

I feel close to Sam, or is it curiosity? I've offered him a job, if ever . . . 'Sam's abroad' is anagram for ambassador, so that's his destiny. His world lives by mafia rules, with additives of indiscriminate revenge. He said, 'When you're in the thieves' web, you get a trial, and punishment. They know you as the bad egg that you are,' and if he lives, he'll do us fine.

*

The last night on the course that should secure Enlightenment, I open up those cans of orange paint, some hundreds of them. Looking for more credit cards, stuck to the dingy dottles of dried paint. Nothing.

The guy comes back from Krakow. To be sure he'd come, I'd moved in with his family.

'I couldn't bring the money,' he says, 'as I

had to pay some guys.'

'A joke, this is?'

'Then there was to pay to change the cash, to pay to get it out, to pay the guys – and here's your share.'

'What?'

'It's the balance. Balance. Something you need in life.'

'No games. You must have bought a house, a palace.'

'Of course not.'

'Then a farm, hotel. An airline.'

'Just fuck off out my house,' he says.

'I can't buy elections with this,' I say. He's unimpressed. 'So must it be a coup?'

I come not seeking power but expiation, I think.

*

I think on. 'Roses, roses all the way' – what a genius that guy was, that's what you need to get a following, red roses for the ladies and a bottle for the guys, the big ideas will wait till you reach the capital, and then your time begins, again. And if you lose, the others get to write your story.

*

I consider my speech, revised.

‘It is good that millions will stop being peasants and become whatever they will be. It is good that as we tire of our friends and they of us, that a press on a key will give a regiment of imaginary friends who will never tire or bore. It is good that some conflicts will be resolved, and others have the eternal promise that they will be – if not to everyone’s delight, then at least off the evening news. That some animals and roots will be saved, though others may not be, that we shall feel hotter, drier, wetter than we were in our imaginary. But we shall adapt to that and our new houses will compensate. It is good that people will be farmers still, and firemen and policemen, and will be soldiers too. And then, maybe we should say at this point that, yes, many of us will be drowned and burned and tortured, shot and exploded in various ways, and that we shall survive to die as older if not brighter guys and gals.

But Progress there will be, and Regress will nonetheless save us from Armageddon, some will be left and probably the better educated and more northerly. The bottle that we call our culture is inexhaustible, the strength is up, the taste more cosmopolitan – a frush of raspberries, tang of wild ginger gathered where the Great Wall fades into grass.

In short, we expect more difficulties, but be assured that some of us will see it through, and in the last resort we can construct some passable and lasting, metal or plastic, replicas, they'll do the living, not as servants but as rescuers, not beings forged but beings freed, if not from rust then from mortality. So, live your lives, to the last drop, the sadness comes from dwelling on the minds and hearts of others – which you can't know. The differences you must respect, the cultures, tribal marks, beliefs, the genders fixed and not – all this gives rights, like yours, which make all them, your lookalikes, unique, unlike, unknowable. At best, they're friends, but they too have their life to live, and so you mustn't stalk, threaten, blackmail, confine, imprison, nor just cling . . . Leave them to be, if so they ask. Don't fuss.'

*

No, I can't say this either. The purposeful life? The good one? Where to begin? Who would be listening, who would follow me?

Destiny, feeling guilt for harm done to people we don't know, don't care about.

*

'Lili's a delicate creature,' Shapur says. 'Princess locked in tower – a nasty trauma. Molestation in the family, you understand, now closed in her armour, her unspeakable History.'

'So lover Rick's shut in this fable too?' I say.

'Yes, he's locked in, locked out.'

I'm not involved – not at all with lovers incompatible. The suffering – we're four in a room here, three men, one woman, the worst combination, one credit card between us.

'At least she runs,' I say, 'a winner, or like that Greek that lost the race but won the golden apple,' and I think of that gold card.

'She's driven. All these sports freaks are.'

'You mean, when she goes off,' I say, 'there's devils with machetes chasing her?'

'Of course. The victors are the fearful ones.'

'Football, then,' I say. 'The ball's a

lopped-off head?'

'Naturally, that's how it all began. Communal anger, then when civilisation came, the head became a dog's, a sheep's, lost its chrisms thus.'

'Shapur,' I say admiringly, 'you are a treasure box of wisdom,' and he smiles, 'As counsellor, I know you spit on my advice.' Wistfully.

A guy like me, I think, just needs ideas, whole bunch of them, then pick one.

*

Before you die,' Rick says, 'you'd better have worked out who you are.'

'What's it to you?' I reply.

He dreams off somewhere. He says, 'Life is putting things in order, no levity, no psychology, no statistics. Saying in advance, you're going to make mistakes.'

'I made some,' I say.

'You won't make any more.'

'On the outside, Lili is just perfect,' I say, 'quite a tangle within, they tell me.'

'She's made a start,' he says. 'I see you as, well, not quite man of destiny, you steal too much for that. But expiation, redress – that's the identity you need to stress.'

We're being spiteful, so I say, 'You talk of sin, when here we are – four dried-out gherkins in a jar.'

Of course, it comes back. The bodies dancing the *pizzica* in the trees, men and women twirling and provoking. They were choking, like the Old West, where they didn't make you drop, just squeezed it out, the breath, gave you the panorama, then that lively hands-off dance, relaxed. A spectacle.

3 Leaving

I SMELL Sara before I see her. She says, 'We're to make another trip together.'

I wonder if we must.

'I see you've bought an airline,' I say.

'Guys in Krakow. Scam.'

We're all to go, and Pliny too, to write it up.

'Can't stand that Lili,' she says, 'always on her tippytoes. And Rick. Can't wait to be a cop.'

'Maybe you like Shapur,' I ask.

'I'd better tell you, that I taped you,' she says. 'And he helped. Three men, one woman in one room – the worst of combinations! How you stuck together!'

There is silence.

'Yeah,' she says. 'Those goddamned tapes,

that bouncy whining, on and on. Drives you crazy.’

4 Distant Shores

IT SEEMS the airplane's in my name. I see the pilots giggling, they seem to have a school atlas, and they've colouring pencils. Another guy in uniform sits with them, he seems quite drunk, but armed, so that should reassure.

'You know where we're going?' I ask, and a pilot turns round, a stubbly face with yellow eyes. He could have tusks.

'Shopping,' he says. 'Everyone goes shopping,' and it seems useless to press him, just fill in these immigration forms.

A strange place, this. A pilot says 'Shopping'. There is a huge tent, it's marked 'customs'. There is not much else. A donkey, some kids begging as we jump down from the plane, they kick us as they take our cash, some guys with guns are looking on, and Lili says,

'Don't shoot, it's only cash.' It doesn't look like they want to shoot.

'Where've you taken us?' I shout, but the pilots are giggling up there, and maybe they don't know, maybe you couldn't get from where we were to where we wanted to be – and Shapur says to take it philosophically, wanting to be elsewhere is part of life and time will sort it out, and we could go to somewhere really crass, worse than where we couldn't go, worse than wherever we are now. So, patience, fill in these immigration forms or else we're stuck, here on the asphalt being kicked and moneyless.

*

They put us in a hulk, a holding tank for prisoners, a boat all ribs and rust.

It's question time. 'Let's get this over quick,' the cop says. 'Reasonable gents, us both. Some of my friends are really bestial. Things get put – rammed – where they shouldn't be. Think of poor

Lili . . .'

'Let's get on with it,' I say. 'And Lili will say anything you tell her – if you mess her up, it's your amusement only.'

'No one's troubled you so far,' he says.

'Kids on the tarmac – a kicking. This boat, where you're holding us – a hot box.'

'We must be sure. The kids just freelance.'

'Sure of my shipmates? Naked illiterates in a cauldron? Besides, we never wanted to come here. Cuisine is awful.'

Then I think, Someone must have wanted . . . someone wants to know . . . such a thirst for knowledge, when it's all around. They can't even get the answers right, there is no heresy to catch, no true faith . . .

The guy here seems to know a lot, and maybe someone else is driving him. 'You must want to get back,' he says, 'elections, press, and stealing stuff . . .'

'I don't get off on stealing,' I say, 'though I think, some cash would now be useful – nowhere to put it, though, shoes have fallen off.'

The dead seem to swarm around. As if they smell you. Dead meat.

We think about that a long time.

'It's true,' I say. 'I whiff, but always try to keep some clean bits visible.'

He's getting irritable. 'Look,' I say, 'it's your fault if you don't know how to rile me.'

'You could suffer some quite extreme pain in here,' he says.

'Don't think I'm indifferent,' I say, 'but if you want, I'm sure you'll do it.'

'What is it that you want?' he asks. 'And what do you want not to want it? What will it take, to break that inner law that holds you tight, together?'

I think, A cop with thumbscrews. But if they want us to renounce our quest, we'd have to stay here, in this hulk. Eternal return.

'It's just betterment we want,' I say. 'Nothing wrong there. Maybe too to give you guys a little twist – quite indefensible the things you do. And your poor indigenous! Guys like you paid for harassment. Threats too. Illegal, mostly.'

He's irritated, and he says, 'You should be ashamed of what happened. Back there. And what may happen when you go back.'

'I am ashamed. But think "system, not person". I am the voice, louder than the guns. I repent. So must thousands more, lose those fine green cars, tomato red convertibles, even the Hummers. Let them go on foot, let them say prayers. Let them run like lightning down the track, let them pay fines. Let them honour one another.'

'And you, you most of all?'

'I'm not honourable,' I say.

'Ha, you're scared.'

'Naturally.'

He says, good cop that he's being, 'Can't we talk, sort this out?'

'Absolutely – but all you have to offer is to let me out, and that you cannot do.'

'I could get you packets of detergent. And some undershorts.'

'Washing in salt water? And it gets real hot in here – your ship is sinking, pressing out the air, sun is an angry god, all day and night . . .'

He sighs. Then someone else comes in. A little guy, 'bad cop' with spots, a little bag of stuff to make me squeak. The game goes on. We want to leave, we should have gone elsewhere, and no response will get us loose, unless they change their minds. For, as Shapur says, if you've the power, it's questions that you've got, answers are quite irrelevant. Once you're caught, your knowledge isn't worth a hoot.

The little guy says, 'Well, I've a problem. You're quite a find. Most of the guys we get through here aren't worth snot.' He waits for a response.

'I can't find the word.'

'I might try twisting your friends, to make you talk. But maybe you don't know anything.'

'You're on to it there,' I say.

'Shapur's a trimmer, that means balance. Balance means sorting out the eardrums. Rick – keen on order, so we might just straighten him some more. Bit medieval, but it's odd how much of us is curved.'

'Kant made that very point.'

He looks angry, and here I am, on a ship of fools, moored in the breaker's yard. He muses:

'Or there's Lili's legs.'

At this, I do react. 'Don't you have something more technological? Besides what do you want?' He looks submissive. 'Betterment, of course. A bit of fun, some masculinity. In a poor country, even torture's cut back to the bone.'

We think of a suitable destiny. I remember 'the purposeful life'.

'Music,' he says.

'What music?'

I know his tune, at once I say, 'Play me Vera Lynn, Xenakis. Also Art Blakey.' That should exclude those three from any music torture.

'I think you're in for Varèse,' he says. 'That's one for sure. How about some Tuvan throat songs?'

'I can't stand violins,' I add.

'Then maybe some Grappelli? See how it goes – the first two hundred hours should shut you up.'

*

And so it came to pass. He didn't break me up, but sent me down my path, hallucinating somewhat, and so sad. Composing my own pain.

Later, I tell the good cop, 'Your colleague doesn't know his tunes.'

'That's really been my job. I would have made your brain turn white.'

'That music,' I say, 'Tickles you up.'

'The Americans send the tunes,' the good

cop says. 'We play them, then we sell the tapes. We have found,' proudly, magisterially, 'after a hundred hours, most any music played quite loud, repeated and without a break, will send you mad. The Greeks were right on that.'

They tell us we have won our case. We're classed as refugees. But it's from here we want to be refugees. No one is listening. We can't circle the globe until our destiny smiles. Those pilots had the right idea, you land where your pencil falls, do shopping from the customs, then it's off again. Stealing my airplane.

'Then where do we go now?' Shapur asks.

'We stay here on the prison ship, but with our status changed.'

'We must have rights,' he says, and Rick chimes in, 'I saw a guy, he had a clipboard, and—'

'Yeah,' Lili says, 'we should find that guy who's got some rights he's handing out,' but it's too late!

They break that ship. What luck! It's our

turn now, we're crouched down in the bilge, but they're aloft, with torches and the whole glow scene, off comes the decking, and the pumping stuff – and we are free!

*

I hug Lili, and she squeals, 'You hugged me!' jumping back.

'Nothing sexual,' I say, but I hear muttering: 'pervert'.

'You should know a guy like you's too old to have a hope,' she says and on my lips I see the words – like 'solidarity', 'glee', 'protection', and I spit them on the floor.

'I hope you remembered the credit card,' I say to her.

'I knew there was something,' she replies, but she laughs.

In any case, no one here takes credit cards.

'In just a while, we shall be issuing our own,' I say.

‘It’s not all suffering,’ Lili says.

‘I’ve never heard anything so fucking silly in my life.’

‘I mean, it’s not just killing and torturing.’

‘You wait,’ I say. ‘You’ll see. They give you a little coin, maybe worth a nickel, and you flip it. Live, let live! Or off with their heads. Don’t be fooled – that’s what it’s about. I want that coin back – they’d no right to take it.’ And I think: No right to hide credit cards in paint, messy business.

Shapur mediates. He defends me, saying, ‘The Boss is still sore because of all those dead.’

‘Someone had to go,’ Rick says. ‘It leaves someone else to tell the fables, in a rocker, on the stoup, knitting a bead blanket.’

We all agree, it’s quite circular – just toss the bad guys through the roof. Now, watch it! – here’s another bad bunch, up through the floorboards. Maybe this time, it’s us!’

*

The place – the capital, I guess – the usual dusty street, with shacks and signs and embassies, and matrons sailing by, with nose jewels. Matrons sailing by, with plastic nose beaks. Plastic bags, full of rutabagas. Lots of little boys, and guys with nothing doing, wishing they were somewhere else. It could be London, Paris, or New York. We see some steps, and I sit down. It's sticky, and I think 'tomatoes', then I see the sign, 'Do not sacrifice animals on these steps.'

*

Before the cops had left, a quite superior person visited, and turned the music down.

'We rather see you as our Opposition,' he said.

'But,' I said. 'But I just want out of here, besides, I haven't any clan or relatives, or network, all that stuff.'

'Exactly so,' he said. 'You are quite bright.'

'You got elections, fair dealing, all that stuff?' I asked.

'Of course,' he replied.

Hearing 'elections', the two cops brighten up, 'Yes, yes,' they say, it is their dream.

'If we are favoured,' the head guy said, 'then the big cheeses say, "Here are fair steps towards democracy," and if they're once more pissed off, it seems we're "pretty backward and corrupt". But things go on, the needle stays right in the groove . . .' and so it seems they need an opposition guy, more of a statesman.

'I have some friends,' I said. 'I've made a lot of promises. There's a tobacconist back there, I said he could be ambassador. And then there's Sam, when he's abroad, he's an ambassador for sure . . .'

'Naturally,' he said, 'we honour promises. But that guy Rick, well, you can't have too much security. So there's a spot for him. Shapur – the same goes for advice. Advisors to the Prince – an army of them, that's called pluralism, so that's him sorted out.'

'And Lili, little runner?'

'She's most important,' he said, 'part of that symbolic authority, charisma stuff. Pity she's not a star, or maybe you could marry her, a romance at least . . .'

'I feel protective,' I said, 'but my role's Olympian. I'm there to give her light and purpose, nothing between the sheets,' and of course I'm trapped, it's power and politics and all those deals, and I added Pliny to the party.

'What's he do?'

'Writes letters, butters emperors with panegyrics, draws some maps.'

'Sounds a good staffer. Any others?'

I thought of Sara, and her tarry teeth, her tart and tarry tongue, her bottom banged away from riding in her Hummer, and I thought, 'So now goodbye, no visiting angels here,' but then the head guy said, 'The Embassy – the big one – have an operative, prepared to drive, give covering fire or smoke screen, help with the shopping even . . .'

'They must have thousands of them,' I said, 'women smokers all – I can't romanticise them.' But she will come, her presence gives us pain.

*

Just being Opposition head sets me to thinking and composing – maybe a manifesto, starting off, 'We all want motivated lives, all the religions promise this – some with conflict, mostly not – and faith should be the ending, not the starting point.'

Then I see, whatever religion these people have, sidling from stall to shack and back, and is it maize or rutabagas, cost maybe a cent to cart it to a matron's kitchen – all this sailing up and down the strip, it must mean everything to them, I just can't dismiss their faith in who knows what – as goal. They have such petty means, they must start off from faith, or else they won't get anywhere, lost on the road. How lucky I could pay, or borrow – that Enlightenment, with food, that they can't have.

*

We talked about our quarters, and the head guy said, 'You might expect a palace, but it takes too long to build.'

'A tent then,' I said, 'but that is ephemeral, and awkward when it rains. You might just call it "marquee" and that quite kills the aura,' and he said, 'A small flotilla, maybe of armoured vehicles – they often fill a void. But if you'll allow, I'll show the perfect digs, that also gives a sense that it's not permanent.'

He led me out, he led me back. The sea's just weak and watery here, like all the seas, and blue and grey and starting over, over, up and down. I told him so, as along the shore we drove. The trees were browned, I though of Agent Orange, how almost everyone but me, remembering, is dead by now. We see – our prison ship again. The deck has gone, but there is ample space for hanging underwear and sleeping on the ribs. Next door, another ship is further gone, beached whale-like, broken down, reduced to song and compass.

'To do for now,' he said, and simpered, preening.

*

The news about the ship depressed my court.

I say, 'We'll have to beautify, so they don't break it on our heads.'

Now, I am on fire, I rant, 'We need cash, an army. Cash is my province – maybe Rick can buy some thugs.'

'I've no money,' he says moodily.

'Just hire them, let them think of ways

they can get paid. As for paramilitaries – find some uniforms. There's an old opera here – must have armour, all that stuff. See if they did *Aida*, that means quality arms – *Elektra* comes to mind, and *Ubu Rex*. They're made for us! Dress the guys – there's *Tosca* too for firearms, and some pikes and such, maybe you'll find a cannon, dry ice will do until we get the teargas. Make a show!'

They stare at me. 'The dealing I can do myself,' I say. 'Let's quit the rackets for a while, we have to make some friends who're clean and pure, no matter what they've done.'

'Even Americans?' Shapur asks.

I think again of Agent Orange, like it was a spyman sowing death, and say reluctantly, 'They've got a great incline towards forgetting. Then the guardians of the memory: they give the job to historians. Well, if you don't remember things, the last guys you go to is historians. Maybe a doctor, or buy a memory book with puzzles.'

Lili just stands there, polishing her legs, mantis or grasshopper, hard to tell.

'And you, whose body is just fuselage,' I say, 'untouchable in motion or at rest – look at these keen and skinny guys, look at the talents in the street. They'd beat you in the ten yard dash, some run up mountains just to herd the goats.'

She looks downcast. 'We only run against other women.'

'That's your excuse,' I say. 'In any case, the women here are having kids and carrying water on their heads, I think you have no rivals there. What you might do, is make a group of supers, call them supernovas—'

She interrupts, 'Like on TV,' and I am irritated. 'No, people with a public presence – aspirations, not envy, exceptionality, not ordinariness. A team of wizards – forget their bodies, think of the fantasy. Magic, Lili. Painting in many colours. Throat singing, if they must.'

*

Sara, of course, is here. She hasn't shipped her Hummer ('Oh, it's coming, it'll come'), but she's hoping Pliny gets here soon.

'Great letter writer – he'll write to all the ministers, even the guy they call the Chief, who made the statues on the way to the capital. Statues of himself, of course. I don't expect a lot from him . . .'

'We're racked up,' I say, 'abandoned in this prison ship, this hulk. They say they'll sort us out, find a new category. But which? As immigrants we're hopeless, we don't want to work or take refuge – we want to go home, run our country, not settle here. But all we've got's that airplane . . .'

She chuckles. 'Ah well, those pilots – pirates, maybe! Will they sell the plane, or take it shopping round the world? As for you all – plans change, that's what they're for. And you could pass for black, your ancestors give you a returnee role.'

'We want out,' I say.

'I'm sure they'll find a use for us, for you,' Lili says. 'So many things to sort out, wrongs to right—'

I shout at her, 'You fool!' . . . and then, 'I'm in control, still in control. Everything has a reason, is effect that's tied to cause, like dogs on leads. The causal chain goes on. And on. It can't break, it's the great chain of reason.'

'Well, I thought – four in a room,' she says, 'the dead people, losing the airplane, all that.'

'It's true,' I say, 'Some things return. Like – now we're four people on a condemned ship. But think of those scalding plates that make it up, think of them as finest suit of armour.'

She laughs. 'They're rusted through.'

'Be thankful,' I say, 'breezes will come fresh to us. Our teeth fall out – no need to share a toothbrush. I'm still the key to this charade!'

She's quite forgotten being called a fool. 'I see you as an old confidant,' she says.

Is this the moment, then, to warn her? What may happen? Leave it to the chain of being and non-being.

They're breaking up the ship next door, cut off the skin, they're at the ribs, they use a crane to lift the dripping organs out, the pumps and motors, all those wires, and then they find the anchor – is it cross or crescent? – and on the heap it goes, with all its chains. Partitions, hatches. Pools of rust, and orange, always orange, paint – that smells of pilchards. Pick, pick, the cranes – like crows. That grey crane, or was it heron, seen from the window as the light, Enlightenment, was coming. Catch the big agile learnèd fish. Light from inside. And now the skeleton alone is left – this ship, undone, is all aglow with orange light. The guys, the ones with welders' lances, they put heat through the system. Then it crumbles.

*

This ship is finished, going nowhere. Only when broken will it rise and sail again. It used to hold maybe five hundred people, who once had souls, a culture, reasons to complain, to flee. To look for purpose. It's months now since their last underwear was thrown away, and in their place we wash our salty clothes, discretely naked, till they're dry enough to dry on us. The sea is orange here, like mango juice.

'Your running down the track,' I ask Lili, 'does it do anything for anyone but you?'

The question puzzles her. 'It's fun, inspires, diverts. It tickles the bone that says, "me too, once", "my country", "lucky her". Then, no regrets, forgotten. And you, Boss? Sitting in judgement? Balancing the purposes?'

'I let the lifesavers save lives, and sell arms to make it harder for them. So, more meritorious.'

'People want that,' she says.

My father kept the first store in the village when it was like paradise, I think. Things to buy, not barter from our neighbours. Objects desirable, giving work a sense. Yet it was a company store, promising heaven, but pointing out you were in purgatory.

'We've serious problems to consider,' Shapur says. 'How to pour sweet words in friendly or indifferent ears.'

I look down the dusty street, the little boys are kicking up and down a plastic bag with something dead inside.

'This place can't do a thing,' I say. 'They've cut down all the trees. Maybe there's stones to sell – I thought that was a joke, but seems it's not, the new tech's made with mud from battle zones, we all go ape for bits of sand. After all, there's nothing here for us that foreign guys don't ship away . . .'

'Those rutabaga things they eat,' Shapur says, 'maybe some policy could sprout from them, some green shoot,'

I stop him. 'We'll promise our new friends,' I say, 'that we're not here to build new dirty stuff, or sell the mud. We'll tell them, that when cars are gone – they never had them – donkeys will be back, and in a million years the donkey fossils will be worth! Then when the friend tobacconist comes, ambassador or commissar, we'll send him off to conferences, with epaulettes. Some opera medals too – remember the dance number from *Traviata*, we'll kit him out somehow. Then just sit here and be an opposition. Can't be too hard – there's four of us.'

*

I go to see the Chief. A guy in uniform they use to park the cars comes with me. He's called a salamander – he lives in fire, of hell or coups. I've seen this one, moonlighting at the inn, swift trades for prostitutes and other things. Guy to be trusted, tariffs fixed.

'What should I call this Excellence?' I ask.

He laughs. 'Guy's got more titles than a bookstore.'

'Not Gone with the Wind, I guess,' but know I mustn't josh along, that way you lose your tongue, my tongue's my trade tool.

'Just clean your shoes,' Salamander says, 'my cousin does a brilliant shine, maybe put on a shirt – my sister's laundry's near . . .' and on we go in petty commerce, no joking with a salamander. The Phoenixes – the next rank up – arise from whatever pile of crap they've made, spontaneous combustion is their trick, their get-out.

My little crew, though precious, over-promoted like some sacred, now just sacrificial, cows, seems meagre. They'll go down with the ship – but then I think, our ship won't sink, just smelt, but now the guy is warning, 'You'd better take a puzzle with you, the head guy wants you there on time so he can keep you waiting,' and so we go, I and Shapur.

*

The palace is a prize, and once you pass the tanks and stuff, and nests of salamanders, squaddies playing cards, there in one corner of the yard, there is the Taj Mahal, and over there a little Eiffel Tower. I've caught it on TV, can't wait to see the tiny Himalayas, and a salamander says, 'Would your mate like a go on the swings? It's Chief on chief – or Boss – today, you are much honoured.'

He smiles, and I recall that I'm the Opposition to his Chief, who'd take my tongue and serve it to the next guy, although no doubt he's father to his people, to his kids, who gives them toys they can't work out, and no doubt every evening tears and punishment.

I leave Shapur to swing, and do some deals with a commercial gent – it's of no interest, whatever cash comes in – it's better figured off the payroll, besides, it's all a net or network we may need when falling off the high wire. I go in and wait.

The Chief calculates his self-importance, worth two hours. The antechamber where I sit has got a droopy tiger in a cage, the cage is broken, so's the beast, I'm curious to see which will give way first – but here he comes, the Chief himself!

Strip off that fine suit, I imagine him as naked, myself taller, clothed. His belly's like a turnip, potted out with sitting on that throne. He stares.

'How red's your tie?'

I answer something, making no jokes, remembering my precious tongue.

'How are you regarding wars?'

Or protecting other peoples, just beyond your border, maybe there's threats and victims – how can you tell? – best put your mothering arms around, and when you think of 'arms', no double take, remember tongue and teeth.

'And order?'

'I have a specialist,' I say.

'You may have heard,' he says, 'there are, ha hum, some areas, areas of concern, I'll tell you frankly,' and he leans towards me, and I get the grave smell, dead things, could be lunch and single malts, or something deep inside, expiring and not telling: tongueless.

'On the whole, we think things should go on,' he says.

'As they are?' I ask.

He pulls himself deep into his throne. 'Haha, a philosopher, I see. That's quite a maze of questions, where you're starting from, where you want to finish up. And do things have a purpose, if they are? And do they change, or are they what they is, or are?' One eye he uses to stare at me, one to point out dingy figures sitting in the corners. So that's his trick. The lizards, some of them, swivel their eyes independently, one for the sentence, one for syntax, one for the hair, one for the shoes.

He's still quite naked, can't be more so, juggling and dropping words.

'How long do we have to stay on that goddam boat?' I say. 'Trouble will come of that. You want a loyal opposition, or a nasty one?'

He says, 'I'll send some gardeners along, to tart you up a bit. The answer is – at most, two years.' There is a silence. Then, 'I've solved the firewood problem,' he says, 'The Yanks have army rations. Cans that self-heat. We'll give those out.'

'For lighting cigarettes,' I say, 'hot soup won't do the trick. Besides, you've got some farmers here, free food won't make them laugh.'

He says, 'Well, either you've hot food, or else you starve. The choice is pretty easy, I'd have thought.'

He looks at me as if I am a wagging tongue.

Later, I ask Shapur, 'A central question?

Things as they are?’

He’s delighted: ‘Singular or atomistic state, particles that dance before the hive . . . He’s a schoolman!’

‘Or else? One nature or many?’

‘What did you answer?’

‘Nothing,’ I say. ‘Asked about the digs.’

‘Excellent! He doesn’t know if you’re up for grammar games! Loyal opposition or pains all round.’

‘How was your swinging?’ I ask.

‘Interesting guy. Very,’ he says coyly.

‘We’ll have to meet the other courtiers,’ I say. ‘Your shadows.’

*

I break my promise to the tobacconist, if he arrives – but after all, the world is round, you stop off anywhere and then slide on. No embassy, but the job of setting off the fireworks at the parties when the Chief achieves the climax of the evening. My friend, my rival, a monstrous banger – he loves his parties, never call them orgiastic, all is proper, watch the rockets.

Thinking of embassies, I had said to Sam, 'I think I want to do what's just. But what is just for you? Trial or assassination? Then, who tries you, and in a way, I see the point of those that's after you, though surely you did what was just. But you are renegade and traitor, enemy, unwanted mediator. The accusation's right! What were you thinking of?'

Sam was annoyed. 'And will you seek out what is just? Or – just votes? Who'll bring you justice, like you think you mete it out, who'll thank you for your being just, and what's the justice for your crime, and for the dead, the dangling ones? Where will you find it, justice? Not in yourself, your feeling bad and guilty – in who else, then? With other rules and purposes?'

'Then, what do I believe in?' I asked. 'Why do I seek a purpose, and atonement?'

'It can't be done,' he said. 'For justice is a

different thing from punishment – perverse to seek it, and it doesn't change a thing.'

*

I don't tell Shapur everything the Chief had said.

'We all make mistakes,' he muses, 'but there's no collective blame. Or forgiveness, either. Each one and only one is subject – crime, mistake, misguidance. But nothing's changed by one repentance, one atonement. Yet only one by one does anything have weight and substance. This moral stuff, it only counts as one by one. If then we ask, what sense has this, when face to face with history – some? none? or start again?'

'In a country, you're all in the same club,' I say, 'waving the same flag, digging the same trench, all that.'

'That's obligatory.'

'Then they shouldn't do it, knowing where it leads.'

'You're rather a shit, aren't you?' he says.

'Besides, things don't lead anywhere – I do.'

'Maybe the key answer was,' Shapur insists, 'at most, we're here two years. Not "when we'd move out somewhere better?" – but "how long can we last?"'

'My gardens,' I say, to lighten it, 'my swinging gardens will be in bloom by then.'

'Gardens? In the dark? What fantasy is this? And what about the other opposition guys?'

'They move on, as indeed they should. No one's immortal, indispensable. The Chief will send his gardeners, then I shall be master of a – of the – garden. Religion, now. There's something moving here – I should look into it, read the book, see if there's paradise or "just keep on the right side" . . .'

'There's no book,' he says. 'Just Speakers.'

'Sounds primitive.'

He laughs, he scowls, tells me to think of opposition, but I'm arranging things and planning – maybe I should be a Speaker. With elections too, and criticisms in the media that I can answer to. The insults never hurt, but sure they're good and cheap to plant. Perhaps I'll put to rights the heat they have here, make sleep easier at nights.

'Shapur,' I say, 'this whole continent's always been too hot. A little tilt, maybe, import some penguins, skiing, all that sporty stuff.'

He laughs, he scowls, we laugh together, as there's nothing to be done, except perhaps we'll hire some guys to fan us on our mattresses, and that resolves the problem, you don't need a book, nor word, nor even grammar, to work that out . . .

*

Hot soup. Was it carrots or tomatoes? Orange, for sure. Surplus from Operation Dragon's Teeth, now renamed Hot Soup.

I organise my little army – politicals, philosophers, good guys and victims. I let them tell their stories, and so we'd score – maybe seventy votes.

Millions spent on soup. You didn't need the firewood. Or the market. That soup – you couldn't wash in it, or reasonably do your clothes. It cut out lots of mediations.

Sara, apologetically – 'We couldn't stop them, I'm afraid, they made an offer for the cans, and heaps of treaties too, and anyway . . .'

'You're well behind both sides,' I say, 'Our lot because they're victims, theirs because they do things,' and her little mouth gives out a smoky smile. 'You're a big boy, you know how it works.'

I nod, say, 'I'd rather not be here.'

*

The garden! In the hold. Those varieties of mangrove, white blind monkeys, then the purple creepers, and the pots where booze is seething, and the flying mice, the perfume – like underwear well steeped in ambergris. The fronds that sprayed above, and triumphed through the rusty deck, the blossoms blue, the white like ice-cream balls, the flowers that spread at night, closed like stripy marbles at the dawn. A place of memory and wonder. The birds that sing like guslars, of heroes never lived nor died, songs of expulsions, cleansings, songs to break your heart.

And now, we slept, we slept so fine, slung up above the mud, dreamed dreams of circus wonders, of jungles thick with topaz, ruby, of insect jewellers, tapping out their marvels. The others said I'd made a paradise – a pity it would sink or smelt.

*

I love my garden. Whatever I am, I should have been a gardener.

*

A guy comes to see me, 'We have plans,' he says, 'For incursions,' and I think, oh no, it's bombings, guerrillas, kidnaps, all of that and more. The trouble is, he's right, and so is who is backing him – *who* I certainly don't want to know. Neither want to know the guy.

I don't tell Sara, though I'm sure she knows, rebellion, secession or crusade – it's in the logic of the place, the story's hardly new.

'We're thankful to you,' Sara says, 'just for being here and doing nothing much – you help legitimate the Chief. So, we'll protect you, but of course – no violence, stuff like that, a statement does the trick. . . And how is Lili's circus coming on, and Shapur's stealing all he can, and that is in the story too, we don't expect you'll live in poverty, there's lots of guys that's trying that, it doesn't work. And do you want a ride?' she finishes off her speech.

'No thanks,' I say.

I think how all this ruling stuff is easy, it's growing mangroves in the dark is difficult, this brackish water, all the monkey shit – you wake up in the morning with the stink, the monkeys fumbling through the leaves, the mice are at the fruit. And yet – it's paradise.

The street has lost its interest, gardening's the thing. The guys are shooting craps, or looking for some scam – sometimes I go to see the ministers, our ghosts. May, shadow to our Lili, organising the culture and the dance. October, who's their Rick, drilling with combat sticks. And February, who's like our Shapur, counsellor to the Prince. The months they represent – the dates, I mean – come from ancestral pasts. Those Russian revolutions, Edens without snakes or apples. Edens fresh and clean, unclothed.

Some guys are striding up and down all day, religious types, they read the book aloud, they've massive cloaks – maybe the curtains from the opera house, cut up. Or maybe stuff imported, warehoused – you often see amid the scrabble for a can of this or that, a labarum, an icon cover – highest quality. Payment in kind, I think, stolen from somewhere, upcountry. Robes, real uniforms, old parchments – even the guys to wear and read them, casting around they are (like us), looking for exits, things to do that don't cost much.

*

The Chief decides to hold some sport. The 'primitive Olympics' they are called. Up to the temple, back down to the airport.

'Just running,' says the Chief. 'And wrestling, maybe, in mud, like on TV. And sacrifices. Makes it more authentic, though personally I've never seen the point.'

An orchestra arrives, they're booked to do some Haydn, but the trumpets and the timpani are lost. The musicians find a bar, and there they stay.

'I'm not running with no clothes on,' says Lili, who's our hope and champion.

'I think that's what the Chief desires,' I say, 'but if you won't, some other streak will win.'

'Don't care, it isn't worth it. Those orchestral guys are getting very loud. Don't want their lurid singing as I breast the tape.'

I'm sure that's the image sparkling before the Chief.

Rick is firm. 'She has a right to keep her shorts on.' There's another right I hadn't clocked, but surely he is right.

The Chief has lost some aid because he had to cancel – he had hoped to bring a load of asphalt in, and Sara is quite furious, the Hummer's suffering from dirt roads, but there's nothing to be done.

So, Lili gets invited to the palace, and as a recompense she dances on the tables, naked as a nail.

'Well, goddam it!' the Chief says. 'We ran the course next night, me and some friends, after the curfew. In the moonlight.'

*

'Notice how the Readers of the book are winning, against Speakers,' he says later. 'Tradition losing out to text.'

'Friendly gods bow out, the threatening letter lands.'

'Yeah, your goddam Pliny's writing to me,' he says.

'He's not here yet, but when he comes, he'll draw a map, and write you an encomium.'

The Chief's perplexed. 'What? All I hear is human rights and prison food. So, what's his skill? Just letters?'

I think: My skill – is all in gardening. Extreme gardening, with animals – moving into insects, parasites, and rusts, funghi, the lesser poisonous creeping creatures. Nature, with all its armament.

'Just call me gardener,' I say, not answering him direct, 'seeing things grow instead of wither. This governing stuff – just backgammon with living pieces, deal them around, you win. Then, there's always some guy wants to beat you. And they will, elections are for that. But gardens – if they die, they're dead forever,' and I think: Oh shit, I should have kept my peace, now he's got news of me he never would have found. He lets the information steam and seethe.

'We very few!' he says. 'Ambitions unrestrained! We don't want cash, security, applause. We don't need people. In any case, the people's happy putting tribes together on the Net, and making friends. Just friends. And what of enemies? Aren't they the dynamite? Pepper? The disloyal ally, turncoats and trimmers – types we cherish, types who make up our trade. Think of those old dictators, making fools of everybody and themselves, doing such silly things, gross, cruel things, and paranoias hanging out. Ideas like teenagers have . . .' He sighs. 'We must do down the Book, and for the while, we're allies of the

Speakers.

'We are the curious, intriguing. We are the real. Persons. We are we, could be our slogan. More modestly, perhaps, I am I, and everyone respects, defers.' He pauses.

'Meanwhile,' I say, 'the hot soup comes, you can't stop that. Nor yet the guys that bring it.'

*

The garden hums with life, non-human.

'If you see strangers, shoot them,' I say, when Rick comes in.

'That's not like you.'

'That is the cleanest way. Besides, armed business stalks around. Some guy, some ship they say will come, that's full of tanks – we have to put some stake into the pot, to show we're on alert. Remember too, the Speakers aren't our friends. The Readers – maybe.'

'It sounds quite complicated.'

‘No one is innocent till they’re gunned down,’ I say.

He looks puzzled, but I suppose he goes to fetch a gun.

Then Lili says, ‘My circus is a gem. May has a trick, she ties her arms in knots, it’s all tradition, so she says . . .’

I’m irritated. ‘That sounds to me like treachery. What the fuck you doing with that May, our enemy and your competitor?’

‘We runners always make good friends,’ she says, ‘until we race, we’re sisters.’

‘Then just pretend it’s “after”,’ I say. ‘Stick to your magicians and the masks, those goddam drums – and mind, no sacrifices, animals or human, no ammunition, keep those weapons simple – sticks and knives.’

She pouts. I know that Rick has contacts with the other punisher, comrade October, though Shapur keeps away from February, them being in business parallel – advice and stealing – both in their ways legitimate skills, not one without the other.

*

Pliny needs light by day to write his letters, do geography – it's mostly diagrams of who is down or up, Readers and Speakers, chancers all. So, he's aloft, just underneath the webby deck. Rick fires throughout the night.

*

The garden is not paradise, it's only plants. It's not a garden cared for, just a wilderness that's loved. Loved just by me. I truck the plants and animals in, the poisonous things come by themselves. By night, Rick's flashes catch us, frozen framing as we wake, and maybe someone on the quay is hit and drags away.

There was a guy, a refugee, we let him sleep down near the mud, the roots. At first it seemed a joke, us refugees who have a refugee, but now I'm not so sure, and Shapur says,

'You're making errors. Showing your hand. It's his, the Chief's, ship that we're in, we're compromised on every side. That's why I'm thinking of a savings plan, to hide a little capital, for if and when . . .'

'But hiding's not my game,' I say. 'For if you hide, you disappear. Besides, the things are multiplying, now guys with guns, the Book – we have to keep a foot on all the things that move. Remember too, the life with motive, purposeful! After the purpose, only then, can come regret, atonement. Without that purpose, we do just what we do. There is no judgment, and no history, we don't know "did we do it right or wrong"?'

He sniffs, and says, 'It sounds quite abstract, things in any case will happen, you cause them or react to them, or both, and so it goes, and on and on.'

'The place is warming up,' I say. 'We need to know – is it to be a burning in the barrel?

Running? Getting out, and to another loved, familiar, even more precarious place?'

He's unconvinced. 'It's always getting hotter here, until it rains, then mud. Then how we long for dust, and some years it won't rain, it's just our destiny. The message? – watch the clouds!'

*

I make another error. Rick shoots almost every night, and then he shoots a lot.

'Use scatter shot,' I say. 'Or maybe ask their names.'

He laughs, no scatter shot's been seen for centuries, and after all, it's character and attitude, and mostly purpose – and not names – that count.

At least he can't arrest the guys and question them. I notice too, the Chief is mean – he won't arrest, and if our little band protests at this or that, he isn't moved, he's not provoked. And when a big crowd gathers, just by people swarming round and getting curious – he's not disturbed, he has them chased away, but teargas is not cheap, a stick will do and as they run away, sometimes they fall and there is chaos, stalls are looted, someone's car is torched, and Rick comes up and asks me, 'Is this your dialogue on rights?'

'Don't twist the rhetoric,' I say, but I wish we had some motorways and skyscrapers, maybe a Reuters office, place to trade, a place to pray at certain hours, a place where you could demonstrate.

'Well, that is how things are,' Rick says. 'Handle your weapons carefully, the people here can run like water.'

It's he that starts to run the game, and I must pull him back.

*

Pliny calls down, 'A guy – could be a friend to see you. Or a thief. Or spy.' Pliny sits up there, a secretary bird, busy with papers and accounts.

We talk about purpose and our destiny. Lili assures us she's found hers, and Shapur nods, his weight of wisdom bends his neck, but like all wisdom it is just to do this or that thing, one will make a chaos or a victory, the other, you will never know. Two keys to paradise garden, and you're allowed just one to try.

*

'We're fine here, though we're immigrants,' Rick says.

'I had relatives here,' I correct him. 'Some the tide casts on the shore, others twirl off to some dump, a purgatory of cork and plastic, spiral that twists but does not suck. That's what we're in.'

I think of Sam, his story ending always round some corner, do you hug the wall or risk the highway – so, we chat along, until – there's Pliny on the lookout. 'Mind, he's coming near, and silent.'

Rick has got a gun, though if it's Doctor Death outside, we should be better in the dark below.

There's an explosion – do I hear a cry of 'holy shit' or something quite inappropriate? – and scuffling off, it could be one in trouble or a few that's lifting loot.

'I can't see a thing,' Rick says, 'but I think I got him, and who knows, but I'm in trouble now. A plot? A friend? Some poor but feisty guy, or horrible, who really knows or cares.'

I think, 'we're in the soup', and laugh, but really shouldn't – those damn cans become strategic. No doubt some guy is hit, invisible.

'Once in a car we hit a dog,' Shapur says. 'Or cat. We never knew, or looked – typology didn't seem the point.'

*

All passes by, and later Lili says, 'The Chief is not a monster.'

'You mean, he's your monster,' I say. 'I can be a monster too.'

'You should see him at the parties, the ceremonies. In robes. And then we take them off. It's the old-time religion, as he calls it. It's very beautiful.'

'I see he has you in his spell,' I say.

'It puts him with his people,' she says. 'They're always in his heart, though as with us, despair is always beckoning.'

She's learned some lesson, and I say, 'There's no justice for anyone here.'

She is irritated. 'So, you must invent some other thing.'

I turn away, 'I don't know why I thought of justice,' I say. 'More cans of something, or else – send everybody back, into the bush to grow those turnip things, just like they did when they were poor but laughed at poverty and died in company, and knew the songs. All that. And what about your running?'

'It's vanity,' she says. 'He made me see.'

'But it pays well. That's what you wanted,' and I think of her white brow lined deep, considering where to hide the credit card.

'It's all a vanity,' she says. 'You reach perfection, you chase it like the butterfly that once you were. Then silence. The speed, the winning . . .'

'That's what you were meant to be, your purpose, destiny.'

'That's so old-fashioned! Almost Greek! It's like your fiddling with Enlightenment! You think there is just one – a steady state – that's some kind of backcloth that shows up well your sitting there and doing bugger all. Be various! Shift that old clumsy shape! Be a monster – then redemption! Surprise us all.'

I feel she's sold her soul, but how much for? To whom? I'd be a monster, though I think

I've been one, and it didn't satisfy.

'Your killing all those people, then feeling sorry,' she says. 'That gives you all the credit you should need.'

When I hear the word 'credit', I think of all my plants, the creeping things, the slime of life that's turning into butterflies. It makes me sad.

I can't take them with me, I think.

'The Chief did let me run,' Lili says. 'In fact, the running was the point, for if you run and run, the demons never catch you,' and I think my strength lies in my running faster than my demons, even though poor Sam is running too, and probably won't win that race.

*

My poor friend too, who died of poverty, running from punishment, his crime was undisclosed. Sam too, I never hear from him again, not since the shooting in the night, as if his ghost was laid.

*

I see us all, us runners, hearts under stress and legs about to pop, and there's no public, just a mass of tracks with other runners, shouting, screaming, winning, panting, and expiring. Lili is first, of course, and Rick is there, the starter with his little gun. And some are finished at the start – and Shapur is trading something, maybe for a better start, and Lili says, 'Yes, the Chief's my monster, but he knows how to be loved.'

What nonsense, I think.

'I'm leaving,' I say.

'I'll get the money,' Shapur says. 'But we've lost that plane.'

Rick is doing well with shooting, plans at least a small battalion of guys who're even keener on justice and its products, so he'll stay awhile, though Lili cries, and says, 'My circus, the traditional arts, all that! What'll we do?'

'I'll not be ungracious,' I say. 'There's the

tobacconist to think of, Sara too, and if she wants to ship the Hummers, that's a headache, can't drive two of them towards the sea – but she's experienced and so, she'll come on with my monkeys, can't leave those blind ones, and the mice, maybe in cages for canaries, and we'll all come home. Maybe while we've been away, the motorways have come, back home, TV with some Boss, religion too, I wouldn't wonder, bit of forest for the indigenous, and stuff to make their phones work. You shall see – it's all in order. We shall have a last performance of the circus here. Then, Lili, you can take the best and worst, and all those opera costumes too, whatever else you like. I'll go and see the Chief, he'll get another candidate for Opposition, some guy got out of jail who's not too keen on going back, should be ideal until . . .'

We all stand there like hunting dogs, our ears are used to gunfire in the night, it doesn't worry us, but now by day there is a crackling, dried wood alight beneath an emptied pot. Or like the ping-pong sounds we heard a while ago.

'But why?' asks Lili, now she's over tears.

'I'm tired of all these poor sick people,' I say, 'the street with Hummers up and down, the dust, the kids who sort tin cans and want to go to Oxford, do heart ops. Should be realistic, think of Harvard, maybe get the Chief to sub them. Speakers and Readers, have it all sewn up, nothing we have can give them satisfaction, let's just get out, like all the rest. Let those who stay know market forces, just like us . . .'

But Lili waves the credit card, and I remember then we never made our own, maybe we'll print and leave some millions of them, good for a day of splendour.

It seems that I've not rooted here, and sure I've not been in a giving mood. With luck and my Enlightenment, I hadn't brought a lot. This old ship, that once exported timber, maybe it was slaves, remains, and in it – now, my plants will die and rot, and at this thought I feel a tear.

Poor plants.

Poor ship.

*

Sara the unkissable: ‘I’ll get the monkeys through customs for you.’

Lili won’t be consoled. ‘You’re not young enough,’ she says to me, ‘and you’re rather squalid.’

‘I never thought of you like that,’ I tell her, ‘for sex, I mean,’ but maybe that’s not true.

*

There is no atonement, just eternal return. Pliny clings, up in his tree, but will descend and leave with us. Sam? Sam’s dodging his assassins, maybe they'll get tired. Or have they struck, the first of us to run no more?

Thanks, Shapur, that bag of cash supports ambition, though I took my Enlightenment on credit. The guys here will stay poor, though someone may get very rich and fearful. The Chief does what he does quite well, he has some sons who'll maybe do it rather worse.

My garden couldn't match his Taj Mahal. But he has love. My love went to the trees.

Those trees. They cut the dancing bodies down, and then the guys back there put on their feathers, gave the final send-off.

Rick will ensure some order, maybe get a uniform that isn't from the opera. Sara is behind him. Everything else – just happened.

5 Back Home

BACK HOME, at the airport, questions, some answers. Usually the journalists, when they interview, tell you the questions first, so you don't stammer or start shouting. Here we all, we few, returned from exile, we stand at bay, me, Lili, and Shapur.

I think: I'll have to call Rick home, this pushing's got to be controlled.

'It wasn't exile,' I say, 'more an impulse of self-disgust, reflection.'

Shapur's pinching my arm.

'How's human rights out there?' someone asks.

'Not a bother for most people,' I reply, then some girl in spectacles complains that the ancient monuments are falling down, what do I think, an international scandal, what's the tourists going to see?

'It's true,' I say, 'you're very well informed, there's lots of ruins. Trouble is, there's nothing from the last two hundred years that's worth the visit – even the big Chief's palace is full of replicas, and rather kitsch at that. It's quite like Greece, the oracles have gone, the temples serve no gods – who anyway are all cast down. Unless you're keen on dust and hi-rise architecture, there's nothing new to see. They'll make you rutabaga stew,' I add.

'What's your next move?' asks the brightest pressman.

I can't say, 'Conquer hearts and minds. And maybe meet some common people,' but I say it anyway, Shapur hustles me away.

'If you get where I'm pushing you,' he says, 'the only common guys you'll see will drive your cars and wash your socks – so leave the hearts and minds to me.'

We scuttle off, I think our suitcases are lost, but Sara will be there and sniff them out. I ask Shapur,

'What qualities in me do you plan to push?' and though I'm clinical, I'm keen to hear.

'Well, you're brave,' he says, 'foolhardy goes down well, you talk a lot, you've read some books or potted them, you're perky when it comes to Lili – and most of all,' he pauses, 'when you've lost, or made some error, you don't care too much, and up and running, just like Lili. I'd call the pair of you The Runners, but it gives the awkward sense that somehow it's escape. What they used to call *fuite en avant*.'

'Yes, yes,' I say, 'I know the tag.'

He thinks again. 'Your greatest beauty is – you're flawed. The people love a flaw, though they'd prefer success. We'll push the "wounded hero" side, as you pant up the slopes, then, once you're at the top – behold the Man! You can unveil yourself, do what the hell you like.'

The Press has asked, 'how many votes you

worth?'

I thought. 'There probably will be mine, Shapur's for sure, Lili if she feels, Rick if he's here, so that makes two for almost sure.'

I confessed to Shapur, 'I don't have substance, don't belong to trades or groups. Don't own farms or banks, or anything that you can't touch, pack up in a suitcase. The other guys, over almost all the world, they're big men, looked up to, fawned upon. If they don't like you – watch your rent, or testicles, or some such other thing you never even thought could hurt, like desert wars and doors kicked in. But I – we – we've got our clothes and not much more.'

'That's your appeal,' Shapur said. 'You represent the little guys, and so they trust you,' but he didn't sound convinced.

'Puff yourself up,' he said, 'and you'll look twice your size or more, and so do down the rest.'

*

Even our little rallies are a show. I stand on this old cart, two tired mules keep it a little jiggling, as if we're nearly off to somewhere. Three dancers warm us up – 'No nudity', says Shapur – but cotton puffs is nearly nakedness. They stamp and reel, I want the dance to be to Woody Herman, his big band: 'Caldonia' – it gets the right mood going.

Sometimes I use my skill at falconry – to have her nip the dancers' puffs is rather kitsch, and often there are hecklers, even someone with a gun. I aim my bird at them.

Some gal in the crowd will shout, 'Your grannie was a whore,' and I scream back and shout her down. She must be some cousin I don't know. Then, when I've boasted of the change I'll bring, some guy will shout, 'It's capitalism you want. Along with socialism,' and we all laugh, the guy's confused, all that stuff's dead, unless there's miners here. I guess it all sounds preachy, but I speak as if I'm voted in and holding court, distributing a job or two or maybe gifts, some jeweller makes them by the hundred, not worth much. There's a fuss if they catch you selling them.

As I speak, the chemicals take hold, some from inside and some from what I take, and we lift off, and as I do some scenes from plays, we all change shape, we join like noble blobs of mercury. It's brotherhood. The guys, the audience, start to look like trees, with animals all hugging round, climbing, leaping, and there's celebrities in palanquins, threading through the mass with crowns and uniforms, and sometimes gifts.

We can't go on without the gifts, and then the mules stride off, we're gone as if we've never been, we're legends, no one's got hurt, or even kept in mind the stuff I say.

Yes, this is brotherhood! I've found my skill, sometimes I remember to bring my falcon home, and sometimes not – it stays to pipe, up in some tree, and that is all that's left of me.

'So, was I great?' I ask Shapur, knowing that I was.

'You are our winning card,' he says, 'our king of swords', and I think: Better than the hanged man. Still, I'm great, Enlightenment has passed from me to them, and back again.

'It was illusion,' Lili says. 'That "all power to the workers".'

'I was talking to that woman, my heckler,' I say, but she goes on, 'The workers work, the rulers rule. And gets paid. It should be clear.'

'Well, as you say so.'

'As for that woman, she was curious. The guy too. Odd-looking, like you are. But that's all gone by.'

*

Sometimes we have a party, celebration.

'I love getting clean,' shouts Lili, running, running, white legs flicking round the Tower of Silence, up to the loggia, sleek between the pillars, pausing at a balcony . . . What will those musicians play? I see a bandoneon, some Chinese fiddles, a soprano warming with cicada sounds.

Lili is naked now, and there are other athletes, men and women, running in circles, round and countersense, it could be dervishes, the light exploding into twirling giddiness, though their own gaze is fixed upon a point, the point from which light comes. Lili and her friends – their eyes are closed, and yet like bats they don't collide. Somewhere below there must be notables, praying or getting drunk, and maybe all will end in purification, or in sex – a scrummage – or in sleep and prayer and dreams of being someone else who's not alive and so – this is eternal life, but not eternity.

'Being clean,' she cries.

I would believe, but does this mean that she's no clothes, no make-up, or she's thrown away the drugs that make her run so fast, so tirelessly? In any case, it's magic, purity, piercing the shell of matter, so easy, leaping over what we see, like horses over logs invisible, their heads pulled up, away – to some fixed point, painted horizon, frozen.

*

Among the notables, I see Shapur. The name Shapur. Something to do with Manicheans. And a fire that purifies, destroys, cancels, evil reborn eternally then burnt away, destruction that is hell and hope. Shapur. Protector of the fire – though my guy here's a chancer, quite as ignorant as me, like me, of parents jumbled up. Should give access to magic of all the cultures, panorama of heavens, gods and goddesses of every rank and power. Blood and soldiers, priests and sacrifices, thousands digging holes to stuff the flesh below. Should give insight...

But it doesn't.

He has an old stone face, features called beautiful because they're tended well, too well. Symmetrical, and signifying nothing.

He even has a bodyguard, so Rick is back. Perhaps the Chief is here.

'Is this an orgy, then?' I ask, and feel I'm crass.

'The usual mix,' Shapur says, 'bits from TV, and some from memory,' it fills some need – that I don't feel. You just join in. Besides, the drink is free.

They're all around us now, the naked and the masked, the naked ones who smile, the others – those who pay, expecting some return.

'Go on, say something,' Shapur says, 'you represent all these guys.'

'I can't represent them all,' I say. 'The ones who give their votes, but not the rest.'

'No, no, it's everyone,' he urges. 'To be legitimate you must include them all, minorities and enemies, every cat and dog.'

'I can't,' I say. 'It doesn't make sense.

Besides, these guys won't do what they don't want. And if they want to go to war, I don't.'

'So, then you must resign – or have a victory or two,' he says.

'This modern stuff,' I say, 'it makes no sense. We're all separate, we don't obey – yet I'm the one who must!'

'You're supposed to – but see what you get away with,' and Rick slides out a thing, is it a fish, a trout? – no, it's a steel persuader – from his coat, and winks.

'We got you in this job,' he says, 'because you're swift, but know fuck all, no other job would suit, nor pay so well to follow you and fawn on you. You're so bright, you understand it all – you climb the tree to get the golden apple – we're still down there below, sawing at branches, mining roots.'

'It doesn't seem to me that apple's gold,' I say.

'Well, someone's got to strike gold soon,' he laughs.

And Lili's there, a splendid thing – who'd want apples, even made of jade and bronze, when you aspire to Lili, giggling. I think I see her mouthing, 'I want you,' but no, it's just a stupid cry 'Speech, speech!'

Slight corpsy smell, from all these dancers, their clean bodies on the edge of steam, a stew of goat and onions.

'What should I say?' I ask.

Shapur's annoyed: 'This is inauguration, purity – not opening a motorway. Think of your ancestors, think of the temples, altars black with blood. Think of the magic, pushing through the curtain! Worship! you turnip. Speak, inflate them with your breath, divine and lofty. Remember, they are not your friends, ladies and gentlemen, none of that! They are the vessels you must fill, you are the Jupiter, your semen boils, they see you there, majestic, metres tall, scented like a bush, hungry for human sacrifice, thirsty for some freely given human blood . . .' And on he goes.

*

'In Brazil,' I say, 'there was a famous challenge, *A Tonga da Mironga*, a kind of war cry, that got made into a song. Should I try an incantation?'

Shapur is unconvinced, but says, 'Go ahead. Anything not too white.'

But as I throw my head back and begin, naming the tribal deities, the cries that summon them, and as I see the figures, like buried sticks, freeing themselves from soil and roots, clustering round, I see the long, dead chain, of all of us who's ever been, knowing what we know, and fear, and love. As all of this begins, and as my eyes look at the sky but see the earth, the sacred ground, the chain of being – it strikes me: they're white, those naked runners! They don't belong here. I'm only a half, the marginal who is almost – almost a piebald freak, maybe a shaman's helper, and they don't know at all what the fuck I'm saying, and they think I'm drunk, or being that dead pop star who made his name with zombies, never made out what it amounted to . . . My spell's not understood.

'I'm screwing up,' I say to Shapur. He leads me off, quite kindly, making a pacifying sign to reassure the crowd.

So, off they go, to run some more, and maybe tangle with each other. Risky behaviour here, it occurs to me that I've got nothing to make the party go, not drugs, a piece of truth or even some fine mystification.

'There's nothing I can give them,' I say, and I'm sad, because those gods I summoned didn't have much reassurance, nor grave goods, nor eternal life. It was all emptiness, unless they sacrificed you – worst of all. Or best. Or just part of a servant's job, buried alive. In the contract, even in large print.

'Nothing is expected of you,' Shapur says, 'though it would be nice if something did transpire,' and I nod – there's some invisible accountant adding me up who now subtracts tonight.

'Where've they all gone, everyone?' I ask.

'Screwing in the bushes,' says Rick, and giggles nastily.

Lili too.

*

Later, at a loss, I say, 'That was a very English evening.'

Rick and Shapur stare at me. I add, 'It's colonialism,' and Rick says, 'But the English didn't colonise us.'

'Then what, what now?'

'You should start a movement,' Rick says. 'Stir things and people up.'

'Miners?' I ask.

'No, of course they're always cross – and always underground. No, you must take the mass and make it rise, like dough. Puff yourself up – it's all about you, after all. You must make a structure – I always think of anthills. Queens, few but potent, and the workers, well, just working away. And whoever else – building, eating what they eat.'

'You're making it sound trivial,' I say.

Rick says, 'Well, once it's done, that's how it sounds.'

*

I think I'll make a show for Lili, I feel I hadn't done too well last night.

'Let's give our atom bombs a whirl, I say.

We've only four. A gift. You can't do much with those. At first she doesn't want, but then the thought of driving round . . . The guy that keeps them doesn't want to put them on the truck. I talk him round – there used to be detachments here, of guys in lunar suits, but then they thought – who'd want to cart those bombs around?

*

Well, I did.

I sing a little, ‘Oh, the active life’s the life for me.’

‘I thought they were round,’ says Lili.

‘As you can see, these aren’t.’

They’re quite shapely, tall, someone has painted pink girl faces on them, stuck on some golden curls. They’re like country maidens going to a ball, they hop a bit as I rev up – ‘I should have been a trucker’ – and we spin along. Some kids are staring, some old guy waves what may have been a flag stuck on a stick, and generally the populace is quite inspired. It makes a show, and though they didn’t pay for them, it seems their right to see what we have got. For a while, the boredom shrinks, I say,

‘Boredom, to Schopenhauer . . .’ but Lili’s restless and she asks, ‘Won’t we get into trouble?’

‘I had a whatsit counter, now it’s broke,’ I say. ‘But I believe there’s stuff in there that lasts a thousand years. There’s history in the future! If it gets into you, you’d last at least two hundred,’ but she’s tense.

I hope that she’s enjoying it, and we are two top dolls!

‘Music,’ I say, ‘we need music, and here’s a tape,’ I put it on, it’s old Thelonious, ‘Straight No Chaser’ is the theme, it seems quite apt, some cops are here to hold the crowds and maybe break a skull or two, but no, it’s clear today is quiet day. I kill the tape.

It seems that Lili’s quite impressed, although she says my driving’s poor. I ask myself what exactly it is I want and can expect from Lili, perhaps a daughterly affection – the type’s ‘old satyr and anomalous flirt’. Or something more mature? The rich old guys I know, the powerful ones, fine art collectors all – they can bestride the age gaps, have some lovely girls who’ll surely be recycled. Some guys get off on widows, especially if they're 25 and wealthy, and so I muse . . . We put the bombs back into store, the guy is nervous, but he's pleased.

And no harm done.

*

'There's been complaints about your show, campaign,' Shapur says. 'It's sexist.'

I'm amazed. 'It's homely,' I say. 'Vulgar, perhaps, but full of Latin culture. Lots of extra, global stuff.'

'You're supposed to defuse conflicts.'

'All this voting's calculated to defuse. You're supposed to get accustomed to it.'

'You didn't do so well,' he says, 'with all those dead.'

I'm piqued. 'I wasn't elected!' I say. 'Besides, we'd all like to spare the good and nice guys – if not everyone. But once you've made that fatal phone call, that is it. After, you can apologise – even change sides, or blame some other guy, or circumstance, or bigotry: misunderstanding on their part or yours. Or principle, the rule of law, let history be my judge, all that. "They should have talked, resigned, converted, stopped blaspheming, downed their arms" – the list is very long, Shapur.'

'I know you're sore about it, but the justification's late.'

'I did the right thing,' I say, 'just turned out that it was wrong. I helped to kill my brothers, cousins at the very least – but now I'm up and running. Metaphysically, not at all like Lili. Running for atonement, I. Victory too, of course.'

*

'You've got to make friends with this General guy,' says Shapur.

General Diaz looks as if he's lost some

power somewhere, now searches for it in the corners. He deals in lines of men, not tribes that tend to circle.

'You must draw lines,' he says. 'The line. In the sky. And roads and railroads. Keeps us safe, in order.'

'Lines in the sky?' I ask. 'It sounds shamanic.'

'Airlines,' he says. 'We've some of those, but mainly roads, we find it keeps the primitives fenced in, the money that we make is useful for our friends. And costs you nothing.'

'Those primitives, my friend,' he says, 'they're murderous. You go up there, you'll find you won't come back. Besides, we're not Big Cap. We own a lot of things, can even paint your house and fix your patio. You'll find us cheap and indispensable.'

At least you carry lots of guns and tools, I think. If we run fast we'll make it through, my instinct being like the tree's, to bend before the wind.

He cuts me off, a word, ‘helicopters’, he’s right and I am done. You can’t outrun those tinny birds.

*

The Chief pays us a visit. He’s in full stereotype, maybe sussing out a future refuge.

‘You guys still running?’ he says, and laughs. ‘Shapur’s running you, you’re running for something, some office, some licking. Rick’s running after trouble. Lili – the only real runner of you all.’

‘We’ve not been standing still,’ I say.

We both laugh, as if I’ve made a joke. Some day, we may be partners, or even enemies, it pays to be polite.

‘But nothing’s happening here,’ he says.

‘I’m making use of my Enlightenment,’ I say. ‘We’re all lined up, the race is on. Pliny, Rick – and even Sara – we’ve all matured, the history time’s clicked forward, some hours have struck. And you?'

'That orange soup is finished. Then, for a while, the whole system seized right up, we thought we'd died. We'd burnt the trees, the animals are gone, there's only us to eat. And then! Then we got by. First, with slum tours. The whole country seemed a pustule, though some ranches held, and of course hotels. The golf . . .' and he sparkles.

'But then we started finding stuff. We dug for roots and found a treasure – every kind of useful stuff in holes and drifts, the very roots cured sicknesses without a name. So, now we mine, we brew and stew, open up clinics, all the curing stuff. The medicines are trickling down. It's quite a boom, we're full of tiny capitalists, and though the situation's dire, I think we'll last. Your ship has floated off, the plants all died, of course, but then, in death there's life.'

I'm surprised. 'And all we do is run and run,' I say, 'and snuggle with our friends!

You'll see, I've plans too, to make us rich and free.'

At the words he nods and lilts, as if it's some old song, and then I hesitate. The plans will come, but just for now – I haven't thought of them, and so we pass an hour, quite diplomatically. He smiles, we smile.

Shapur joins us. 'Your months – February, May, October – seem quite auspicious,' he tells the Chief.

It's empty talk, and Shapur says, 'This guy,' he points to me, 'I fear he's too baroque.'

They both pause wisely, the Chief smiles and says, 'No harm in that. You'd not believe the stuff that we get up to! The rule is this – don't worry about consistency, don't drop all your eggs at once.'

I'm irritated. 'This Shapur guy,' I say, 'he's made me leader of a fascist bunch.'

'You'll find the house has many rooms,' the Chief says, 'and some smell worse than others. But they all communicate, all do business. People pick and choose, they wander up and down and in and out, like us. Don't go cold on life, my friend. The people like to see us having fun, so long as things go well.'

I think of his parties, climactic fireworks, all those billboards.

'I love myself,' I say, 'but not as much as you do. I keep it all just "me to me",' but he has turned away.

'They think it's up to me to make their life a happy garden!' I hear him say. 'I've my problems too, but no one thinks of that.' The two of them, arm in arm, they move away.

'You bastard,' I scream, but they're far away. I'm full of words, my rights and wrongs, they fill my throat and won't come out. Still, I want to be like them, but maybe better, or more lovable, or just more fiercely pure. So, I scream again, perhaps they walk a little faster, still arms linked. I look for things to throw, but everything's screwed down – security.

Screaming doesn't seem to serve.

From afar, I hear the Chief say, 'He had the ship for two years. I'll charge him rent. Even under water.'

My fear is not the Chief, the General, prison, exile, the lash. Today, my fear is that one day, to help my cause, reasons of state, I'll owe a kiss to Sara.

I know about the Chief, the General – the thefts, the whores, religious scams. The tortures, all that stuff. I know the guys who'll take their guns, to do them down, and then the thefts, religious scams. I am not cynical. For sure, I'd do the same. But there is more to power than what they call abusing it. The Founders had it right – pursuit of happiness. That's the deal!

I flip my coin, so fast the legend blurs. Freedom, equality, fraternity. It's like a butterfly, a humming bird, a dragonfly, it's like a prayer wheel whizzing round, a dragon's scales a-sparkle, a fine sword showing off. It's like the evening's close, the guys are drunk and you've held forth, the twinkle of the coin – it's whirling now, not dervishes but space is fizzing, round they go, the faces, like petals, scent of irises . . . it's happiness! You'll get nothing more, and nothing better. This is your cosmic patrimony, so drink it down, don't count the bottles, turn your pockets inside out, and let it come, the happiness, keep on coming! There's no 'enough', no 'home now', you'll never tire of this pursuit . . . Happiness! That's my project, my eternal plan!

'You have to care about these powerful poppies,' Shapur says, 'their excesses – or at least say you do. Take them as part of nature, also yours.'

'Excess!' I shout at him. 'That's our programme, don't you see – it's what we promise. The power we'll keep, but spread the happiness around . . .' and I expand on this for days.

*

I go to see my blind white monkeys, and they stare, stare at me without seeing, but so touching. And those flying mice, coupling in middair – thousands of them, millions, gobbling up the stuff that we can't eat, like falling leaves and little buzzing things. I'm delighted, seems I've solved the puzzle. Happiness, abundance. All the other stuff's quite useless – guys that knock the buildings down, the money that collapses, viral meltdown, inventions that explode and make you live in fear. All vanity, oh, just vanity. The spinning coin slows, droops, drops. It's heads.

*

Pliny is here to do PR, to puff me.

So's the tobacconist, expert in puff and drag. There's Sara, she too making smoke. I think: We've got all the useless ones. Sara is full of 'too much too soon', and 'our friends' here, 'our friends' there, probably she's paid to steer us on some track. It doesn't seem that track is straight and true, nor penetrating like the General's, but all the same I think hers ends up just like his.

'You need them all,' Shapur says.

'No, I don't need anyone,' I say, 'I never will. I'll find another ship, or, since we have no sea, a steamer from the lake, and plant it out, call it an ark. But it won't sail. I, and the beasts, some Indios if they will do the gardening – then, on the beach we'll found our little state, no votes and no majorities.'

'How will you live?' asks Shapur, laughing.

'We'll eat each other, just like you,' I say, dismissing him. I find I have this gift and privilege – that guys are pleased to be sent outside when I've been shouting at them, maybe I'm preachy but it seems to work, to get some peace.

*

The Chief was right, he said to me, ‘I know exactly how to run my lot, until they decide to snuff me out. We rub along, it isn’t pretty, but each day it makes the sun rise, then it sets.’

*

My plan is bigger. Flipping my coin, it seems to say just ‘brotherhood’, fraternity. That will do for my first term, so Shapur says, but I’m impatient and we’ll do the lot straight off. Lili will help me with her circus acts, the guys that stamp their feet, with bells, contortionists with feathers, and I think: Maybe I’d look good too, with one of those grand wicker crowns, maybe a beast inside and birds on top, and Shapur says not to be gross, respect tradition but don’t bow to it. I think that’s bad advice, but I hold back the great ideas, to let them out like racing dogs, once the landscape's clear.

*

'Everyone loves you,' Shapur says one day.

'I'm flattered,' I reply.

'Loves you, but they'll dump you just as soon.'

'Love all of it? Of me?'

'The gambling, exile, truck with bombs, even the monkeys – yes, it's all come good. Everyone identifies with some of that. And they hate the other guys.'

'So,' I say, 'Just "to mine own self be true" – that's it?'

He seems offhanded. 'How's the plans?' he asks.

'Day after election, if we're sure I'll win.'

'Well, of course there are, there were, the dead. But they don't vote,' he says.

I flip my coin again. '"Freedom, equality,

and brotherhood." How's that?'

He smiles. 'How long do you propose serving?'

'We'll undo the latifundia,' I say, 'out with the guys that own TVs and all that stuff.'

Patiently, he says that everything must take its time, and so and so, not to be rash.

'Well, we have good black credentials,' I say, 'also brown, some of my friends are this and that, and I am half a Muslim. Thanks to my grandparents, indiscriminate screwers that they were . . .' I gallop on, and Shapur tugs my reins.

'I heard you're Zoroastrian?' he says, 'So where does all the rest come in?'

'A fine poetic creed, that one, indeed. A special place for animals too. Remember, I'm the great gardener—' I start off, but Shapur interrupts.

'No irony, no sarcasm, forget your jokes as well. Don't use them. Don't let it seem you're in it for the cash.'

'You forget, old friend,' I say, 'I took Enlightenment. And Art. Besides, I won the lottery.'

'You haven't got a cent,' Shapur says, 'we'll have to find you lots of bucks,' but I am off.

'Lili will do the culture,' I say. 'Rick controls the crowds – each of them will have a court, that's how the cash comes in, many hands, you know,' but Shapur's on about the mouths to feed and already the venture's turning sour.

'For me, the power is all I want,' I say, 'not glory, medals, all that stuff.'

'We need to have a General,' Shapur says, 'things are toughing up . . .'

'No, no to wars,' I say. 'I cannot stand that stuff, all looking solemn as the corpses pass, then off to Europe, cadging arms. That's not my scene – I'm your creative type.'

I think of installations in the hills, the runic verses. Lili dancing naked in the temple.

'No war,' I firmly say, and Shapur writes it down.

*

Then – 'Enlightenment works!' I see it. 'I have grasped the light, the centre. Shapur, you know we have such things as – global culture, global economy, suchlike?'

'Yes.'

'The idea is this. The "Banquet for the end of the world". We all, everyone, sit down alongside, all together – murderers, torturers, thieves, priests, giants, the moribund – all of us. Capitalism creates itself, creates more Capital. It's quite indifferent to greed or goodness. All it need is guys with power to keep on feeding it. And to them too it's quite indifferent. So what we'll do is – have a banquet! Eat all we can and want.'

'It's a terrible idea.'

'You're wrong!' I say. 'It's the Idea. I've

even got the slogan – wow! Banquet for the End of the World. Loud and strong. Get it?'

'What'd we eat? Meat?'

'No, I think – leave the animals out. It's not their thing.'

'The menu?' he says. 'Everyone wants different things – then they complain. I've been to some of these displays.'

'Details, Shapur. You fix.'

'The indigenous,' he says, 'they don't sit down to eat.'

'They used to own the earth and sky,' I say, 'but now they're used to being given just a little back, a sliver at a time, and being photoed while they're enjoying it.'

'I just don't see the point.'

I flash my coin at him. 'This Liberty – there's all the problem. Will, power, culture, ties that bind, the causal chain. We know what we want to be, we've doubts about the others. Then Equality – well, no one wants that! So that leaves Brotherhood. It's a last chance.

New World. Or end it all, annihilation.'

I see it all. There's Lili, dancing on the tables, Cape to Pole, and Pole to Peshawar. And Rick – his goons will see there's tranquillity with the booze.

'The cash,' Shapur says.

'The banks like spending it,' I say. 'They'll find us lots. It's ours. For them too, new start, or end. Dead end. For many people, it will be the first and last great feed. We'll stake all our resources. Paradise regained, or nothing. If it succeeds, we won't have Paradise where everything's prepared, laid out like a dream, snakes and ladders, punishment park. When we've had our feed, our pig-out, in the New World, there won't be tables laid, musicians tuning up, and Lili stripped. We'll have to start it all again. But with that glow of Brotherhood . . .' and I speak long and hot and high, with my gift of tongues, tongues the banquet will keep wagging. Brotherly chat, subdued, quiet save for the soft percussion of the jaws, sweet *portamento* of the stomach.

*

Shapur is running hard, I'm floating high above him. He tries to pull me down. 'It all sounds, well, teleological,' he says.

'Forget the long words, Shapur, they've no place at our table. Besides, what's wrong with a little teleology? "Peace, Land, Bread",' I declaim. 'Those Russians had the same idea, but messed it up. I'll put it in one word – the Banquet. Forget "All power to the Soviets" – we'll see if Brotherhood will take us on, or drop us in the . . .'

'Washing up?' asks Shapur.

I'm irritated. 'Trivia. Details. Shapur fix.'

'What's this to do with here, this place, your new career?' he asks.

'Everything. The Vision. The Idea. Who else has that, Shapur? You? Lili? Rick?' and for once he's flattered, and I think: The second string, of Pliny, the tobacconist, they're not too strong. And will the guys with guns drop them at the door, or have them close at hand, under the table maybe, but the thought hops off, too simple to be distracted by minutiae.

I think the Leader of Enlightenment might give me the diploma I'd not paid for, and at last see me as prize graduate. Maybe for him some gift – a whole eggplant, little strawberries.

I send myself a note. 'No rutabagas,' remembering that dusty street, the matrons with their plastic bags. Maybe the menu's something I can have a hand in, but I say to Shapur, 'Details, you fix. Fix them, Shapur.'

I explain the project.

'Great, when do we eat?' Rick says.

'Show us your redeeming feature, Rick,' I say.

'That'll be some fucking long table,' Lili says. 'I'll need new shoes if I'm to dance along it.'

'Who says you'll be wearing shoes?' I say

and I catch them winking at each other, like ‘the old satyr can’t button up his thoughts.’ They snigger to themselves, and I think, ‘Haha,’ for when it comes to thoughts, I know they spy on mine, but I’m not slow to peek at theirs.

‘Maybe Sam’ll turn up,’ Rick says. ‘Now, there’s a real runner.’

I think that maybe Sam wouldn’t feel secure, elbow to elbow with his executioners. There’s a problem, for although events like these produce their dead and injured, old Sam’s a friend.

It comes to me that that’s an anagram too – or nearly so, ‘a fried salmon’, and how apposite! We’ll put it on the menu in Sam’s honour. Then I think: Oh no, we can’t kill fish, especially the obsessive ones. Freedom does and doesn’t mean a lot to them, that swimming upriver, sex all uphill and fatal, programmed in – and on I muse when in comes the tobacconist.

'I guess that means I wait on tables,' he says, but we all feel exalted, even Pliny, though it's all been written down for him, to put straight in our newspaper.

'There's no head table,' I say, which means I don't need invite the other candidates and presidents to sit near me, nor Sara and the team that runs her – though thinking thus, it then occurs to me, that sitting on a mountaintop and eating timbals, chatting to god of sky and wind – maybe that wind and sky's got in my head. For all I'm good at delegating, poor Shapur's 'details' are swelling up like clouds.

'Fix,' I say, and hurry off.

*

Shapur sends a banker, 'to talk sense.'

He's cashmere above and jeans below.

'Aha!' I say. 'So you're the guy! social production, private appropriation – I've read about you.'

‘It’s all confidence,’ he says patiently, ‘your credit card, to take an example dear to you. You trust me to lend, I trust you to pay it back.’

‘The cloud,’ I say, ‘far up there, hovering over the unclimbable summit, is Capital. Sometimes you bankers make it rain a little. We fill our pockets – and the water makes our clothes shrink.’

He’s not a man for metaphor. ‘We make a little rain because we have the power to do it. Or not.’

‘We’ll make a bet,’ I say, ‘remembering that I won the lottery! We’ll see if you survive the Banquet. All or bust, brotherhood or mayhem. Give us the money – the bellies belong to us! The morning after, see us farming Eden.’

He laughs. ‘The workman’s blouse has never served behind the boardroom table,’ and I think: He’s never seen the working stiffs, they’ve left before he’s up.

‘My dear,’ he says, ‘you’re in the confidence industry too, I see. Promises for votes. But Lili – she’s got talent, something solid. I shouldn’t draw attention to her sex, although she waves it high for all . . .’

I say, ‘That’s all irrelevant. Just sign this cheque for money that’s not yours, lay out a spread, put more something in that cloud up there.’

*

Our universe is Capital. We’ll send a probe out, in a thousand or a million years, back it will send the message – ‘opening hours, the Friendly Alien Bank, all loans considered’. But – just let me have my bet.

He just smiles on, and hopes my candidacy’s successful, and I say that Shapur knows the details and will fix. So, off he goes, and Carlo is his name, it could be Boris, Kwame, any goddam name, it’s all the same.

My ship, I think, at least was honest as a piece of work, with fantasy – just like that installation with the orange cans of paint that might have held a fortune, but I go my way and think: Banquet is All. And many guys must think the same, for there is chatter here and there, and sayings on both sides, and maybe one same guy has said he's for it or against it, the same day, we'll never know and, really, I don't care. It's all a competition, if I win I'll go ahead and send the cooks to work.

*

Banquet. So beautiful, held here in my mind, a diamond deep set in a crystal globe. Pity to spoil it, details – chairs of plastic or of wood? No chairs at all – buffet, that stretches on a bridge of rafts, through storms and calms, that rises like the Great Wall, up where there's no air, the god Oesho holding court, then to the Tibetan plain, and on where pandas frolic, doubling back to shaman land, the flags, the stupas, then we come to lands of hi-rise, rigs and roads, then more deserts, millions wailing for their ghostly saints – and then we're off again: to jungle, dusty streets with guys that wish they were not there, and then it's landfall in Bahia, dark city where it all begins and ends, and round and round again and join the chain – somewhere near Tulsa.

The guys will eat, their families too – you needn't sit with family, but families hang on and many guys are proud, or just resigned, to have them. The same with clans and tribes and gangs, you may not like it, but you mostly do, or have to, and the tables are a garland, necklace round and round the world, it's like a set of chains, mostly weak links, I fear.

And maybe Rick with squads of goons is standing there, a watchful baseball bat that's good for sport or keeping all in line – and eating. So, of course, no drugs or booze, we'll have to search the lot, maybe have them sitting there quite naked, like in Eden, so they can't hide a gun or knife, or even take a timbal or a walnut home . . . Because, of course, there won't be any 'home'. That's it. End of the world – or Brotherhood, with us marching in lockstep somewhere new.

I think it's beautiful and awful too. That's where it parts from life as it is lived, the bits you see as beautiful are only so because the rest is not. And 'awful' comes with edge and smash at three o'clock one morning.

*

Later, Lili says, 'I don't like you calling me a whore. I like running about, and dancing. I'm good at it.'

'The price of happiness is unhappiness,' I say sagely.

'Well, after . . .' she says, meaning after the banquet.

'You guys don't understand,' I tell her.

'There is no "after", there is do or die, and "doing" is to be quite different.'

'So, no blisters? No washing dishes?'

'Ask Shapur.'

Better be a happy Lili than a cypher like Rick, I think.

'It will all depend on Rick,' she says. 'If he stops the fights . . .'

'He'll have to learn some new techniques,' I say. 'Usually, when he stops a fight, everyone piles in. It's the male thing, Lili. Not everyone's like that, but put a few million under arms, lots of heads get broken.'

'And when we're strong enough,' she says, 'we gals, we'll show you all.'

'Yes,' I say, to blunt the edge, 'you'll all smoke cheroots. But the Banquet has you all sitting down together, eating, not shooting.'

She's not convinced, this running stuff has eaten into her, it's just she stops at some fixed point, instead of aiming high, at the horizon. Keep on going, Lili – the details will get fixed.

'Of course, all this is fantasy till you're elected,' Shapur says.

'Ah, that's how it works.'

'Lili's now the pretty face of the candidate,' he says.

'That seems quite inappropriate,' I say.

*

Pliny is a big man now. We thought, when we were studying Enlightenment, the two Pliny birds were into mathematics – on the lines, we thought that, 'God is a mathematician.' so perhaps mathematicians are a god. It turns out ours, the Pliny, wrote letters, a slippery art, where offence and rhodomontade lie in wait, you say too much and maybe you exaggerate a bit, you slide from honest flattery to fraud and fireworks. Now, he runs our newspaper, dressing up our news with shots of Lili, on the front as stripper, on the back as winning athlete – in between there's nothing much apart from Pliny's musings, under every name except his own.

I see him as he sits there, his pen is moving like a fly on speed. Our secretary bird, predator's shadow on my lake-bound heron, broken-ribbed and rusting, umbrella of too many storms.

When I prompt him, he says, 'All and any of your news, give it a spin and I will set it down, still spinning. Integrity's assured by coming from your mouth'.

I feel he's forgotten our Enlightened course, distinction made between authenticity and integrity. And no, I don't remember now – the two terms seem so close, uncomfortable. But though guys laugh at how we puff each other, it seems to work.

I shall be resolute with the tobacconist. He's already writing menus for the Banquet. He chalks on, chuckling to himself: 'Fun-guy, Bark fan, Coli-flares, Cart-offals with white sores.'

'I've my doubts about you,' I tell him, 'and you're already mocking my idea.'

He's surprised. 'Little bit of homely humour. Besides, I'm your talisman, I get you winnings.'

That is true. 'I'd never drop you from the team,' I say, 'but remember, Enlightenment is not just reasoning, it's following conventions.'

'I see more winnings,' he soothsays, 'birds are flying left to right, they spell out your name.'

'OK,' I say, 'I'll make you minister of health and destiny, so each one gets a winning card, the biggest prize will be eternal life,' but I shall drop him. It's his destiny.

Shapur's annoyed. 'You want to get rid of that guy? He's a perfectly good spy. And we need him as a medium.'

'He's too stupid for diplomacy.'

'He passes secret information. No information's any good unless it's secret.'

'Secret and true?' I ask. 'But we've no

secrets.'

'Then you must invent some. Otherwise – how do we feed the spies? They follow you around, they're the ones who really wish you'd win, that guy and Sara, the little dragon whose fire's gone out.'

'Everyone will care when I die. Then they'll wish I'd won.'

'That's good defeatist talk,' says Shapur. 'And not untrue. Life is a tragedy for everyone. Sounds absurd, if true! ridiculous – so life's a comedy. Some of us they grieve for, others not. Summarise that – if you or Pliny can. But keep the spies well nourished. In the end, the historians will do their sums. Does that console you?'

Of course, he's right. Historians are always ready with their spades, to open up a grave or two.

*

Spreading out below me, an immense slope. At the top, the Travellers, homeless, abandoned and abandoning. Everywhere there are campfires, bonfires, shacks burning, set by vandals, by people tired of shacks, by bullies from the city. Rituals, burnings and brandings, smeltings and solderings. Below the Travellers are the seamen, waiting for ships to leave or dock, seeking some line of grey horizon, line of amethyst amid the blue, restless on firm land. (We have no sea).

Then – allotments, purple squashes in the half-dark, grasses like finocchio, monster artichokes, things frightening like rhubarb gone to seed, inedible and quivering. Then, on the plain, more fires. It's like the army of the Ghaznavids, waiting to take India; fires orderly and gridded.

The Traveller guy, called Paco – almost all of them's called Paco here – says, 'Take a drink and hear a story.'

'I've no time.'

'It isn't time it takes.' Life. His up and down, his down and up, from factory to workshop, then a period in the street, and then again the working class, then artisan, then helper, half-begging, every interlude with a story. Everything and nothing, trades half-learnt and forced to drop. The other Travellers have heard the tale before. It's theirs. They travelled once, and now they're beached, heavy-laden with their stories.

'Would you vote for me?' I ask.

'No.'

'Then, would you follow me?' He nods. It's dangerous ground, this moving of the immobile. Really, a moving of the fluid, shards of history trivial till you live them, surfaces that never stick to anything.

'Where would you follow me?'

'Wherever.'

Because – the active life is best, there is no other, really. But it's dangerous. Paco's story fascinates, is forgotten in a moment.

I wander through these vast camps, of guys who're tired with what they've done, of guys with nothing particular to do. Men without women, without children, sailors with no sea, travellers with no roads, farmers whose stock has died, the grains all skimped and thirsty.

A group of miners here – they are in work, they're standing in a clump, they ask for news. My head is full, but of Enlightenment. It seems a thin thing. Their heads are full of gods and spirits, heroes and battles on no map. I have no story for them, but at last, I start.

I tell them of the ship, my ship, and how their mine resembles it – the hammering, the fear of drowning under rock, darkness, the going nowhere, just the hollowing out of darkness. I don't talk about the garden and the animals, as those are things they cannot have, and cannot know. I just talk about the ship, the sounds it makes, its voyages, its fellows beached alongside, being broken, fletched and burnt, their souls ripped out, without respect or chronicle.

The guys are silent, and seem interested, so I go on, maybe three hours or so, and sometimes talk of that main street, of cans of paint, of luck, of orange soup, and how it all connects. Or – maybe it doesn't, and I feel them drift away, dreaming of things that I don't know.

Then some guy at the back shouts out, 'The Galleon.' Some other guys take up the shout, and I am sailing now, I tell them how the mine is theirs, and they know that, have always known, the mines, the rivers, lakes, the streets, the little telephones that people use – it is all theirs, has always been. The only question is, how to take it back. It seems to me that now, we, in this battered country, without a sea – we're sailing.

'The Galleon, the Galleon', they cry.

At once I think of General Diaz, of Shapur, of Sara with her lumpy car, Rick with his goons and all the rest, the guys we've bribed for this and that, the press and all that stuff, those rallies – oh, the rallies, and I think: Oh fuck, I'm compromised, I am on every side. Shapur sends to tell me I should watch what I am doing, not to go to the edge.

*

The Galleon's a fine movement, and we spread like well-worn voices, guys in their thousands winkle out their families, if you count them all, they're millions, knowing what they want and how to get it, and I grow legendary, pushed along as if on wheels.

*

'You romanticise these guys,' Shapur says. 'There's lots of criminals, and fickle too, and scum.'

'I'm not a moralist, Shapur,' I say.

'And lots of people could get hurt.'

‘I’m not a humanist, Shapur.’

‘Perhaps not, but you’re squeamish. And your hang-up, about death.’

‘I just look for meaning . . .’ I tell him, but he interrupts.

‘Most thing’s it’s easy to give meaning to.’

I correct him though, remembering Enlightenment, and say, ‘OK, it’s significance I want.’

‘Are you another, wanting to be Bonaparte?’

I say I’m not. ‘I never touched the button, off it went, the Galleon, no sail, no wind, no coal, no anything, it doesn’t veer to right or left, it moves. And doesn’t budge.’

*

Though when I asked, ‘The Indios, the Mayan crowd?’ and thought of Maya who I’d drunk with, of the indigenous, their *pizzica*, then the Travellers said ‘No way, they’re liabilities.

Everyone is after them, the troops, the gangs, they're hunted, hounded off their land as well...' Besides – The Galleon! Don't see them on any ship, still less one called The Galleon!

*

'Sara and the big bosses, they're a tiny bit alarmed,' says Shapur. 'I hope they don't step in, they have such heavy feet.'

'I've no new scams, resources, to add to those that you already know,' I say, and think of the Tibetan letter, the paint cans on the hill, one can that could be still alive. That orange agent that can strip the world of leaves and fruit, just leave itself behind, imprinting, art eternal in the genes.

I say something about avoiding poisonous artifice, which he doesn't grasp, but takes it as applying personally.

'The Galleon is eager for the Banquet,' I say, 'not for the end of time, but so the

Galleon can start its global trip. They don't want "paradise or death" – rather, they know what Brotherhood is.'

Under his breath I hear Shapur, 'Don't forget sisterhood,' and it's true, I'm maybe quite a pig, intolerant too, and bigoted, and quite obnoxious with it. And if he wants to know, I'm proud too of the defects, raising me up, inflating me. They're not the worst of flaws.

'You must pretend to like our friends,' Shapur says patiently, 'who give us money, even stash their arms with us.'

'I'm not stupid. Where'd we put their cash?'

'The credit card. So, seek the right path, don't run ahead.'

'It seems too late to run,' I say.

'Run to compete, not to escape,' he says, and Lili tiptoes into mind, and I caress the memory of the hill, its installation, inert and useless, full of ideas unopened, fortune or blight, and I curse that here I am with withering things, that garden lost, growing and flowering in the dark.

'So,' says Shapur, 'Sail the Galleon with infinite precision, and when I tell you – sink it!'

'Must we?'

*

A million bodies here or there. The scholars wait the call to add them up. Skeletons. Anonymous is better than committed, named. Just enter in some figure with a chain of zeroes, judgement is passed for quantities, your own small life is counted in, dismissed, with all the regiments, your comrades and their pets.

Shapur says, quite kindly, 'Don't dwell too much on your Enlightenment. It really means 'indifferent', casting cold eyes on you, on everyone. It's always been a curse. So morbid. Run forward, like that Lili! Till you burst!'

*

Expansively, Shapur says, 'Shit, but we're lucky.'

I agree. 'Credit and the lottery, great inventions. Trust and luck.'

'Sure, without that, Lili would need clients, Rick would be a bent cop in a slum, you wouldn't have a plan, nor even your hands on atom bombs. You'd be on the corner of some street, dreaming of Milan and riches.'

'And you, Shapur, in tandem with the tobacconist – smuggled cigs?'

We dwell silently on our fortune. 'Don't think of it as fortune,' he says, 'think of it as right.'

Before us is the little patch, the cemetery, where those sad indigenous are buried. There's little mounds of dust, some kiosks selling drinks and nuts. And isn't that a beaver? – maybe a muddy pig? It's quite a primal scene, some animals still tracking through, some guys in feathers picnicking – and look, they're waving, goddam racket from their radio, but all is over, has been said. Settles into anonymity.

Now there's a struggle, two guys setting on another guy who's occupied their space and is selling stuff in gourds – they've done him over well and smashed his bicycle.

'Wherever you go in this place,' I say, 'the past and present, even future – it all haunts you, all is metaphor and portent, you must close your eyes . . .'

When I get my stamp, seal of consensus, what you will, I think, I'll stay away from places like this, that serve for nothing, the little stunted lives, atrocities.

'In the future, only grandiose things, that's all I'll do,' I say aloud.

Shapur says that he approves.

'Fix it,' I say. 'This shallow cult of democracy – the guys aren't interested, or they're cynical. Everyone climbs and no one runs. The scum floats to the top, the people wait for coconuts to tumble off the voting tree, and when their heads are smashed – well, if they are able, they lose interest, or they're cynical.'

'So, what do you want?' asks Shapur.

I race on, 'The armies that occupy and bring democracy to people battered to their knees, throw up some puppet friendly with the generals, some clique, some tribe, some clan, that says it speaks for all. But can't restore the sacredness, of being born a something, rights not just given on a card, some head office somewhere, formality. . .'

Shapur is already walking away. 'You don't understand a thing,' he says. 'You take it all too heavily. You take procedure for principle.'

'The principle's a fiction,' I shout. 'We're subjects of a state that's quite indifferent to who we are until it's time for uniforms . . .'

'Do better if you can,' I hear him say from afar, 'but remember, that this race here's the one you're in.'

I take a bus. I see a fire, some guys are sitting round, it's early yet, they can't be drunk or stoned.

'What do you want?' they ask.

'I want to find the true spirit,' I say, 'spirit of brotherhood, of action. Remember, "Oh the active life's the life for me,"' and they offer me the bottle and they sigh.

Brotherhood. 'It's a prickly symbol, creeps up everyone's nose,' they say.

*

Sara is downcast, she says, 'We're slowly packing up. There's new crowds coming in everywhere.'

'What about your Hummer?' I say.

'The new guys make their own,' she says.

It's hard to feel some sadness, but I do, even the gladiator's death is moving.

'You never took to them, did you, my hopes, beliefs,' she says sharply

I reply that it's hard to feel involved in someone else's thoughts. She looks at me as if I'm strange, but I am an Enlightened man, I let the world do what it does, and what it thinks is far too complicated.

*

'Lots of shooting here at nights,' Rick says.

'Yes. Maybe. I guess. I'm asleep.'

'It's not the guys beating up I care about,' he insists, 'it's shooting.'

'You mean it's my guys, my sailors?'

'Seems likely.'

'They don't like criminals,' I say, 'and they've no money. What do you expect?'

'Nothing,' he says, 'nothing. I expect nothing. The Chief, he was a pretty violent guy, but I would say he treated us quite well. That is, not bad. And we had cover, somehow. Difficult situation, in that boat – but we were good guys, opposition, rights and such, and votes. But here – the sticks are drier, words just hop around and set things off.'

'There's nothing I can do,' I say.

'You should speak up, then we'd send out our guys – they'll take out those little shooters, do persuasion.'

'I just don't feel like it. It's in the culture, I don't care if bad guys get hurt.'

He turns away, I'm pleased he doesn't argue. His guys want order, mine want justice. Theirs is all clean stuff, not torture, burning out the families, all of that, so let's just say it's warriors. Let it run.

*

'Mind you don't bring the tent down, shaking on the pole,' Pliny says.

'Scribble, scribble, Pliny,' I say.

I don't want to win this hand, don't want to lose it either. If the Galleon moves ahead, they'll leave us far behind – and then, who knows?

*

'Ignorance will save you,' I say to Lili, but she doesn't heed.

Sam has written to me – 'I'm trapped in this room. I've no money. If only my murderers would knock, or break right in – and yet, I'm terrified. I'll come and see you, if I leave . . .'

'You remember Sam?' I say to Lili. 'What can we do for him?'

'You could answer his letter.'

'How?'

'Rick has friends who know these things.'

A way of showing Rick he's still trusted – but I suspect our visitor, back on the ship, was our friend Sam. I mention it to Lili, and she's angry.

'You didn't think because you didn't care.'

I didn't care, I think, and so we did for him,

that Rick – he shot Sam on the quay. And so, poor Sam, poor Sam. So, we resolved his fears – assassination at the point of liberation. Poor Sam, his destiny had found him out, a dog's tail it was, always attached and twitching.

'You've gone from being obnoxious to downright evil', Lili says.

'Let's use a word we know just what it means,' I say, but I have done for Sam, my friend. Detail, Rick, Shapur.

Fix it.

*

Lili says, 'That Galleon frightens me'

'You're right,' Shapur says. 'We thought we'd broken up old loyalties, that everyone would think only of themselves. But these guys in the Galleon – they're like Athenians or Spartans, bonded to the death. They can be handled, but I don't know how. They're quite another crew, they don't just hope for paradise, they've got its angels, its dimensions, even the music that's played there. They'd kill the guys that vote against. Even if we go to war, and drop our bombs, and they cheer all the louder, they'll claim the victory is theirs, and carry on! The ordinary guys – they want this paradise, and they think they're going to get it, and the leaders know they won't, but must keep the whole mass moving.'

Pliny is desperate, can't sell a paper. He and the tobacconist are talking strategy, how to sell their views, for every day the Galleon is changing tacks, a new enthusiasm's born, it sweeps them on, the sails fill out like melons, who isn't for it better hold their noise or jump, and there are sharks around – better to stay inboard.

'This energy's a dangerous thing,' Sara says. 'If you can't plug it in to somewhere safe, the big guys maybe will cut off your food and drink! With no more pills and bonesaws! Our revolution's done a while ago, and once for all

– don't you guys start imagining you can do it over . . .'

'I'm not responsible, although I'm proud,' I say and think: that Hummer's a good target now, but really mustn't think like that, and I remember Sam, who should have sat with me and shared some drinks. Our Banquet for the End . . . for great survivors, all those hated by all sides, but muscling through, still running.

'Poor Sam,' Rick says, 'he had a restless soul,' and I don't think it goes to Paradise.

Sam's letter says, 'Your friend, the one they took to pieces, he with no cash and heavy clothes. I envy him, for luck might always fall on him. My luck is in the hands of someone else . . .'

*

Now the gals are coming out and joining up, they're with the Galleon now, they leave the sheds and factories where they make the little phones they use, that plastic gear for cleaning ears, the pants that come apart, and children too – they're tearing up their history books, they're running barefoot down the tracks, leaving the teachers standing silent. My Enlightenment feels quite thin. Am I with them, or bystanding, watching as this river pools and joins, mercurial?

The guys, the Galleon – they've seized me, my name's the one coherent thing they know, they shout it, and I'm part. Leaving the inchoate, up to that happy land they'll recognise, have always known, where people, animals, behave just right, and those who've nothing live quite well and don't intrude. Families – they work together like a set of pistons, and there's feasts and deaths, torrid summers, winters with a flood of snow, but still the food gets through, the kids in school are singing – what? Hymns? War chants? I can't tell – the sailors on the Galleon know, and maybe they'll all want a war, or burn some sect, and certainly some well-set guys will end up on the trees a-dangling, some new song will resonate – and everyone is happy and a little high, except the bad ones who are bumping down to hell.

The Banquet – not the one I had in mind – is in their eyes. They're running on, I hope the guys that's carrying me don't fall, they are assorted heights and strengths. I lurch a lot. I see the tables, going round the world, all those trees felled and irreplaceable, those birds whose homes are wrecked . . . I wish I'd waited, and I see far off – it's Sara, staring as she sees us scampering down the hill, borne on by nothing, no power, no wealth, just gravity and impetus. She's drawing on her root.

I see the Hummer jiggle – over and down it goes. Here there'll be trouble, we've a lot of thrust but not much power. Shapur is on the phone to moderate guys who're sitting on their chesterfields and dreaming – of scaffolds for us, probably, and I feel that while we're going forward all our sins are dropped, we're pure and blessed, at least as long as we rush on.

Lili, I see, is quite appalled. It's not a serious race, no competition, and no finish line. There's just happiness, exaltation, brotherhood. It's frightening. No, terrifying. I set it off, and it's not my Enlightenment.

'You in charge here, are you with them?' she asks, racing alongside.

'Yes,' I say. 'Yes, I'm here and running. Yes, I am the candidate.'

*

I am the candidate. The Galleon doesn't have candidates.

It will sail on (we have no sea). Will there be other Galleons? Terrible sea battles? Where will it beach? I'm pleased to see it sail, away. Some day it will be beached, the crew, of course, be disappointed. But if you take a cruise, a voyage, the ship's the place, there's no finality beyond these planks, and where you visit is just clouds and fluff. The voyage – ah, the voyage! Of course, the Galleon, my Galleon, doesn't move – we haven't got a sea – but still the sailors climb and shout 'land ho', or 'flying fish', 'Vassili – the dolphins'. Here and there, a whale.

Here, I'm the candidate. Damn it.

*

Shapur asks, 'The Banquet?'

'Well?'

'All details. Couldn't fix.'

'Forget it, then. A terrible idea. Without Sam by my side . . .' and we are silent, seeking the right emotion.

'In any case, with all the fights . . .' I say.

6 Power

We did it right.

We nationalised the big stuff. Threats from all sides, old friends and new. We left the managers – who'd made historic profits just some months ago, and now it's all dead loss. The Galleon without a sea is far away, and anyway, ours is not their Happy Land.

I don't read the papers, even ours, though Pliny writes me letters, and some panegyrics. So, I run on.

*

Shapur says, 'The Chief is moving on. That is, he's been moved. Doing all right, though.'

'What's the big change?' I ask.

'February, May, October – their names, and they, are taken off the calendar. They're thinking of Cold, Warm and Cool instead.' He laughs. 'They couldn't call them Hot, Hot and Hot, so they compromised.'

I suppose I laugh too. 'I wonder where our Indios, the real Mayans, suchlike, went,' I say, 'those hanging from the trees. They and the spirits, the nature. The gardens.'

'You know where they went,' he says. 'We saw the burial ground, those kiosks. Besides, they were of no account, just thugs.'

I'm sure that's true, I can't conceive a ceremony for them, begging a pardon, for what I do not know, from whom I do not care.

*

We go to a conference, Shapur and I – the last and only. Some come in space ships, some in pedal cars, some pee down reeds and some don't pee at all. Our photo's taken – start day at the asylum, someone tweaks my bum. There is much talk of cash and actresses, the guys are spouting Revelations and John Locke, some bring their bishops bearing silver hands, others bring shamans naked as herrings.

We talk of everything – of speed limits, dogfood, where it's safe to keep your stash. The little guys are talking up their sex, the tall and gloomy ones seem set on war – or maybe peace, it's hard to tell. We go to eat – there's noisy guys nearby, banging their pistols on the cutlery and talking fast in little telephones that come out of their mouths – and when we leave they try to add their eats to ours, our credit card, saying we owe them. They shout and laugh, 'We're your security', but we escape, into some alley. There's leaders in all the bars and joints in town, and lots of funny guys and gals get licences to export themselves that night, and end up who knows where or what.

'It's just to get on television,' Shapur says, 'be a gay dog, if not quite gay, you understand,'

and I'm quite glad our TV doesn't work too well, problems with generation, something such.

I'm proud of the figure that we make, Shapur looks as though he's not been assembled well. He takes offence at this and sulks. We talk about my garden. It was no eccentricity, I say.

'It grew towards the light – but whether that was up or down, was hard to tell.'

In the night, the corridors were circus time, it brings to mind our Lili, and I think: She should be big Boss, not me.

'The great thing, when you run you run alone,' she's said, 'there's no one piggy-back,' but I'm not sure of that. As Boss, she'll end up pulling carts. Laden with clients.

*

My foreign friends put out the tongue at me, and poor Shapur takes spit, but all in all they won't invade, it's bad publicity, they'll have to bring their food in with them . . . I think of General Diaz, who seems sure that he's the rock on which we perch. I think of Colonel Diaz, who's his son, and feisty Major Diaz, who's no relation, and will plot. We spend our cash on sticks and stones the General's lost or broke in guaranteeing our success. They seem to cost a lot, maybe it's war he plans. Our friends are pleased we've paid them off.

I think: I'll paint those atom bombs with orange paint, to make them scarier still, and then I think, the galleon, its sails so red and green, the sailors skimming along and singing all the while of landfall, breadfruit, noble mistresses that make it all worthwhile . . .'

I nearly miss the vote, and Shapur says, 'Quick, in the alley, I see trouble,' and indeed a bunch of what seem Yanks, Biharis and Chinese – maybe they're allies, maybe they just teamed up, it's hard to tell, they've got some clubs and pointed rods – they're after us!

We skeeter off the scene, seems this always happens when they've had the vote, they pick on some small lands and give them 'something to remember'.

'Put it down to hormones', says Shapur.

*

After our conference, I brood.

I tell Shapur, 'I'm fed up with this. I'm on the move again. That elusive, eternal orange paint, somewhere it waits for me, serene and ugly in its can. My destiny.'

He's dismayed. 'But you've got personal power . . .'

'Vanity, Shapur.'

'The other people. Friends, comrades, partners . . .'

'We gave back what we could,' I say, 'most of that was vanity too. The good guys have stuff to eat, if they will grow it. The guys in "Galleon" are as happy as they'll ever be.

Everyone wants their kids to be doctors and nurses, so we've put the dying off as long as possible . . .'

'And your ideas, if I may say, your ideology?'

'Intact, Shapur.'

'Ideals? Dreams?'

'The same. They keep on coming.'

'Retirement could be seen as cynical, or disillusioned.'

'Fix the papers, then, Shapur. Get Pliny to say I seek "new challenges".'

'Sam would be disappointed.'

'We killed him, Shapur.' That ends the argument.

'My circus?' Lili asks.

'Keep on with it. The only pure and innocent thing. No animals, remember, they don't see it our way.'

*

I say to Pliny, 'No compulsion, but instead of

using "freedom", "equality", and "revolution", why don't you make your paper say how the figures go: deaths and such by violence, famine, and disease. Avoidable and not. Each year. Like the results of running, or of football, a calculus of felicity you'd call it.'

Later, I hear him with Shapur. 'The time for Lili's come, I hear,' he says. 'The Boss is off his peg, and she'll do well, circus is very popular for now.'

'She's quite conservative,' Shapur says. 'I see no sign of tender conscience, just a passion to be first. That suits me fine, I'm safe in second place.'

*

So, Lili steps into my shoes, as I step into Sam's – for running. I scarcely leave a print, but if I do, it's raked out quick.

Lili the lovely, best left alone, untouched. What little profit there would be in loving her, in making love, as if there's something 'made'! Better let her run the show, dwarves and contortionists, leapers, fallers, clowns – the circus is a weighty metaphor that's high above her, though maybe – it could be her soft spot. She runs, she battles with herself. The circus world won't help her to come first, but then – that's culture!

Pliny will review it all.

And for a while she'll run this land. With Rick.

*

As I leave, they start to hunt me. Can't think why, what profit. The General has new guns, I bought them for him, and they shoot up alleys, mounted on slender halftracks, which slide like they're on snow – that we don't have.

*

I buy a big hat.

I squat down in the main street, with my blanket, along with other guys that no one looks at. The army trots, up and down – I'm pleased to see they've cavalry, it always makes a show, I had their stables fitted out.

I see a newspaper.

'Little Boss – scoots – leaves chaos,' Pliny writes and goes on, 'He started well, defending the border with his goons – his first absence gave us time to reflect, even to love. Then the return, the dream, restoring stuff where it never had belonged....ambiguous relation with the Galleon, and even General Diaz . . .' I race on.

'Corruption of athletics, our sweet heroine, the Lady Lili, and the man of order, Ricky, forced to be witness to – approximation, absences...should check his credit card....behaviour typical of gardeners, should let the things that wither, wither, not get all the flowers to bloom, not persist in schemes as worn out as they are utopian.'

Then, 'It seems some atom bombs are missing – not enough to cause a worry. Then too, there's the question of his misogyny,' and it seems I should have put an end to theft, and then I think: maybe he's right, then try to judge how far, how fast, it's sensible to run.

You give these guys – Pliny, the tobacconist – work far beyond their talents, then you see them, on their Hummers, driving round the town, looking for real estate to buy. As for Shapur, where is he, given neither praise nor blame? Pliny's final judgement on me – 'Oligarchy', the 'Destroyer Boss'.

I'm glad for Lili, for the way has opened up for her. Glad, not very glad..

*

By phone I speak to Shapur.

'Pity that you ran,' he says, 'and you will leave no trace. Lili will start from her new line, and Rick will fire the gun. They always need advice, good if it's mine! I hope they won't be suckered into war – that strip of frontier, where they set up the massacre – it's good for mansions, military camps, though it will lose goodwill, and cost a war, but after all, the guys that follow Diaz only have their lives to give or lose, and so will find a beneficiary, nicely public one, wood coffins for real, and lined! Brass bands.

'The tobacconist is quite another case – seems he and Sara, in cahoots, have fallen out. Much talk of bodies, reputations, bloodied badly, dumped in the rubbish. That too will pass. I hesitate to talk to you of ships, of things shipshape, on even keels and such. Some things we can't ignore, however. That Galleon's a pirate vessel. Nonetheless, it is a presence, and will cause, no doubt, some fearful nightmare soon. Meanwhile, I can imagine you, still seeking credit in that orange paint – who knows what aesthetics drives you on . . . those heathery hillsides, dug-out serifs on those runic signs, the rust, abandon – gives me the creeps, and maybe you as well.

'Ever before me are your dead and dying. They are your Agent Orange, that defiler, twister of people, killer of gardens. The ill-fortune that we fear and seek, and cannot deal with, responsibility never to be discharged. With luck, the last one alive among us will forget that special Agent, along with all the other things it's better to forget. Our Saviour gives us all dementia, which is the greatest gift, surpassing even mercy, forgiveness, and atonement. Holy, holy – if I may interpose some words that surely mean so little to you – forgetfulness. You who have sought Enlightenment and put away the sombre, humble things – forget, dear little Boss. Forget, and find another garden, if you can.'

*

Shapur will carry on. Pliny has sold his pen, sold out, will carry on. Regrets from Sara, she won't write but you can hear and smell her all the same. How that Hummer could be helpful now, more trusty than a credit card.

*

The Galleon is sailing on. I hear the cry, 'Land ho! The Happy Land', so many times each night. They never learn the Galleon's the thing, not land nor sea. That's Brotherhood all right, but I am not on board.

If I just scuttle down this alley – that ditch looks bad, so, one foot either side, avoid the shit and stuff, at least one's shoes are clean – as for the rest, keep running on. If you look back, you'll see the cities of the plain implode. Remember, the fault's not yours.

*

I'm proud of everything I've ever done, including my apologies. I have my pride intact.

About the author

John Fraser has lived in Rome since 1980. Previously, he worked in England and Canada.

www.ingramcontent.com/pod-product-compliance
Lightning Source LLC
Chambersburg PA
CBHW020550310726
48979CB00008B/1154/J

* 9 7 8 0 9 5 6 1 4 0 9 6 8 *